Karl Hillebrand

GERMAN THOUGHT

from the Seven Years' War to Goethe's Death

Karl Hillebrand

GERMAN THOUGHT

from the Seven Years' War to Goethe's Death

ISBN/EAN: 9783741123795

Manufactured in Europe, USA, Canada, Australia, Japa

Cover: Foto ©Andreas Hilbeck / pixelio.de

Manufactured and distributed by brebook publishing software
(www.brebook.com)

Karl Hillebrand

GERMAN THOUGHT

GERMAN THOUGHT

FROM THE

SEVEN YEARS' WAR TO GOETHE'S DEATH

SIX LECTURES DELIVERED AT THE

ROYAL INSTITUTION OF GREAT BRITAIN

MAY AND JUNE 1879

BY

KARL HILLEBRAND

NEW YORK
HENRY HOLT AND COMPANY
1880

PREFACE.

———◆◇◆———

READERS acquainted with German, who may wish to follow up the necessarily brief indications of the present lectures, will find further information in the numerous histories of German civilisation, literature, and philosophy, more especially in the works of Biedermann and G. Freytag on the first subject, of Jos. Hillebrand and H. Hettner on the second, of E. Zeller on the third. In the following pages the lecturer has kept almost exclusively to the works of the great German writers themselves and to the following, amongst many hundred, special works : Dieterich on Kant, Haym on Herder, Helmholtz on Goethe as a naturalist, Dilthey on Schleiermacher, H. Hettner and Haym on the romantic school. No fault, the author hopes, will be found with him for having reproduced here and there the conclusions of his own earlier essays on Winckelmann, Wieland, Lessing, Herder, W. von Humboldt, Caroline Schlegel, H. Heine, Gervinus, L. Hœnsser, the Berlin Society from 1789 to 1815, the German Unity Question from 1815 to 1866, the history of classical philology in Germany, &c. &c. (published between 1865 and 1872 in the 'Revue moderne,' the

'Revue des Deux Mondes,' the 'Journal des Débats;
the 'Nuova Antologia;' the 'Preussische Jahrbücher;'
the 'Fortnightly Review,' and the 'North American
Review.')   They were so many preparatory studies for
a general work on the subject, which has never been more
than a project, the author having since abandoned this,
for an entirely different field of research.

K. H.

CONTENTS.

CONTENTS.

LECTURE VI.

EPILOGUE.

LECTURES

ON

GERMAN THOUGHT.

———•◦•———

LECTURE I.

INTRODUCTION—ON THE PART OF THE FIVE EURO-
PEAN NATIONS IN THE WORK OF MODERN
CULTURE.

1450–1850.

LADIES AND GENTLEMEN,—You will readily believe
me, when I say that I begin these lectures with
great apprehension.   It is the first time that I am
called upon to address an English public ; and I
am to address it in its own language, the most
precise and at the same time the supplest of
instruments in the skilful hands of those who are
used to it from their infancy, and have a complete
mastery of it ; but a dangerous one for a foreigner,
ever liable to miss the just measure and the right
expression, weighing too much here, gliding too

B

lightly there, and becoming to a certain degree
the slave of the engine of which he ought to be
the absolute ruler.   I know that the audience I
have the honour to address is, if not a *parterre de
rois,* at least a parterre of gentlemen, and that
consequently it will be as lenient to a guest as
it would have a right to be severe, if it were to
assume the functions of an impartial judge.
Nevertheless, I have thought it my duty not to
rely too exclusively on your hospitable indulgence,
or to overrate my strength in launching into these
new waters without the swimming-apparatus of pen
and ink.   However alive I may be to the advantage
of speaking over reading, I must forego that advantage and bring you my thoughts already made,
as it were, and congealed, instead of letting them
flow and expand naturally from the running spring
of the spoken word.

What renders the honour bestowed upon me
of addressing so select a public more perilous
still, is the consciousness that I have but an
imperfect control, not only of the language of
words, but also of the language of thought, predominant in this country and in our days—an
idiom, I am afraid, which I have still to learn.
Every country and every time indeed has its own

intellectual atmosphere; and a Spaniard who in the sixteenth century might have spoken French as well as a Parisian, would have failed to understand Voltaire or Diderot, if he had come to Paris a hundred years ago, as they in turn would have failed to understand him. Now, I am perfectly aware that the intellectual atmosphere of the England of to-day—which is fast becoming the intellectual atmosphere of all Europe— is not the one in which my generation has been bred and reared. If I, for instance, have lived long and intimately with the English of the past, I know little of the English of to-day, or, to speak more precisely, I rather know about them than know them. In the whole tendency of my mind, in my entire way of looking at things— religious and moral, historical and scientific—I have remained a thorough Continental, nay, a thorough German, whereas the younger generation of Europe is entering more and more every day into the intellectual current which sprang up in this island towards 1860, and has since spread over the greater part of the Continent.

But this will require an explanation which will lead us at once into the subject of these lectures.

We may consider medieval Europe as one vast family, which, for a time, thought that it might *Unity of Europe.* remain for ever under the same roof, and work in common at the great work of civilisation. One language, Latin—one Faith, the Catholic—one Law, the Roman—one Sovereign, the Emperor—were to rule supreme, and shelter all the members of the family. In reality this ideal was never completely attained. Yet it governed men's minds during the whole Middle Ages, and even in after-times haunted certain intellects, which were thirsting for unity and order, but were unable to find them in variety and liberty. The law of nature nevertheless was stronger than the laws of men : Europe outgrew the parental house, however spaciously it seemed constructed. No sooner had every hearth its own familiar language, than those who were assembled around it wished to give vent in that language to the thoughts and feelings of both their every day and their ideal life. From the day when a philosophical thought was expressed in a national language, that division of Europe had begun, which, during the fifteenth century, resulted in the national monarchies of England, France, and Spain, in the Italian renaissance, and the reformation in Germany.

The division, not the disunion. The work which Europe had done collectively and simultaneously till then was henceforward to be done separately and successively, so that, as Algarotti said of his own nation, 'the one who had got up early before the others, and drudged a good deal, might rest somewhat in the day-time.' Nevertheless the work done by modern Europe is truly one work, although the workmen have several times relieved each other, handing on to their successors the torch of intellectual life :

Vitai lampada tradunt.

It is one stock, one capital—the capital of humanity—which they have accumulated, each in turn contributing the fruit of his labour.

I need scarcely warn you, gentlemen, that these and similar expressions must not be taken too strictly. Humanity is a living body, in which every part is intimately connected with the other, where every separation is felt like a sword-cut, painful at once and endangering life. Still, as the philosopher has a right to separate memory and imagination, will and sensation, understanding

and reason, which in reality form the living
individual, so the historian must claim permis-
sion to divide mentally what in reality is closely
united. When England exercised for the first
time the intellectual hegemony over Europe, when
Gilbert and Harvey, Bacon and Hobbes, Newton
and Locke were writing and thinking, Italy had
her Galileo, France her Pascal, Germany her
Leibnitz. Still, for any impartial observer of the
history of thought, the focus of the movement was
in this island.

Italy was the first of the European nations
to come of age and grow impatient of the paternal
Italy,   authority. As early as the beginning of
1450-1525. the fifteenth century she boasted of a
poem in the national dialect, which summed up
the whole intellectual life of the middle ages; and,
a century and a half later, she began to emancipate herself from this very system of thought to
which Dante had given the most beautiful, as
well as the most adequate, expression. The day-
work of Italy may be reckoned from 1450 to 1525;
but I must once more beg that such limits may
be taken *cum grano salis*. Nobody can fix the
exact line where one's arm ceases and one's
shoulder begins; still the anatomist must needs

make the division somewhere. Everybody has present to his mind the events which, towards the middle of the fifteenth century, awoke Italy, as well as those more melancholy events which, seventy-five years later, laid her in the grave, or at least in a long and dull lethargy. You are all aware how Italy discovered,. as it were, the treasures of Greek art and literature, how she cleansed, mended, and made them accessible, and rendered this purely lay and human civilisation the basis of all modern culture. The important point for us is to characterise in one word the nature of the intellectual work accomplished by her in those years of incessant and almost feverish labour. The Italian Renaissance was the re-habilitation of human nature; and the instinct of history has not been mistaken when, up to this day, it calls the representative men of that age the *Humanists*, their culture the *humanistic*. The Middle Ages and Catholicism had subordinated the present to the future, liberty to authority, the human to the divine. They had declared flesh, *i.e.* the natural instincts of man, sinful, and preached the suppression or taming of them. The Italian Renaissance reversed things. For the naïve scepticism of a Lorenzo and a Filelfo, an Angelo Poliziano

and a Marsilio Ficino, the present alone had
reality, and as such it was to be understood, described, enjoyed, as the Greeks of Pericles' time
had tried to understand, describe, and enjoy it.
All that was in nature was good and beautiful, instinct was the surest guide, natural force and beauty
were the truest signs of and titles to superiority.
Let not the fact of their formal adherence to the
Church mislead you any more than their enthusiasm for Plato's lofty idealism.   The Church
was for them nothing more than an indifferent
garment which a man would not needlessly ex-
change for another, or lay down altogether.
Platonism was a form of poetical dreaming,
not a philosophical conviction.   What they
pursued was the knowledge of human nature,
mental and physical, and of human society,
not as they might be or ought to be, but as
they were.   Whether Machiavelli is describing
political life as in his Prince, his Decades, his
History of Florence, or is depicting the social
life of his times as in his Comedies, he never
enters into the question of good or bad; he is
satisfied to understand things.   So do the philosophers, the poets, the artists of the time.   For
them art is what Goethe proclaims it to be, what

our century seems to have so utterly lost sight
of—'the interpreter of nature,' nothing more,
nothing less.

This might have been harmless, as it was right,
if it had been limited to Art and Thought; but it
was the pretension of the Renaissance to make of it
the rule of life and action. Our temperament and
our mental character frame our opinions, mostly
without our knowing it ourselves. It was the sensuousness of their temperament and mind which
especially fitted the Italians for their historical
mission; but it also led them to such lengths that
they incurred the penalties attached to excessive
indulgence in one's own thoughts and inclinations.
They saw everything in the light of art, gave to
everything an artistic form, regarded everything,
public worship, the State, even private life, as
within the province of art; and the thought that
they were living as the Greeks had done justified
everything in their eyes. They forgot that in
Greece 'the Muse accompanied life, and did not
direct it.' What it came to, the names of the
Sforza and the Borgia tell us forcibly enough.

A strong reaction set in—a double reaction;
the one popular, appealing to the inward authority
of conscience; the other coming from above and

endeavouring to restore the outward authority of
tradition and collective force : the Reformation of
Luther and the Society of Jesus. The former,
although prior in time, had its full influence upon
the strain of higher thought in Europe, only a
century later in England, only two centuries later
in Germany. The latter acted at once, and it
Spain,   was Spain which gave rise to this move-
1525-1600. ment. When, ten years after the foundation of the Jesuit order by the Spaniard Ignatius
Loyola, the famous Council was opened at
Trent, it was Loyola's successor, the Spaniard
Lainez, who became at once the directing genius
of that great Assembly which renovated Catholicism by giving it the form in which it has lived
and prospered during the last three centuries. I
find our time somewhat inclined to underrate the
importance of the part played by Spain in the
history of European thought. Of course hers was
above all a negative action ; but she acted also in
a positive way. Not only was the reorganisation
of the Church entirely her work ; the absolute
Monarchy of Divine Right, as it flourished during
the seventeenth century, was equally of Spanish
origin. Think of the difference between the
medieval conception of sovereignty, and the one

which was the soul of Louis XIV., nay, even of
the Protestant James I. of England, and down to
the smallest German and Italian princelings of
that time ; between the variety of the feudal
royalty of the Middle Ages with its almost independent vassals, and the uniformity of the modern
monarchy with its passive obedience and its
l'Etat c'est moi. Now one might say, the monarchy of Louis XIV. was simply the despotism of
Philip II., tempered by the innate sense of the
French for measure and taste, enlivened by their
natural serenity and elegance. This, however, is
only one side of the question, and, for our object,
not the most important.

At the same time that the principle of
authority, both religious and political, received a
new impulse from Spain, and conquered after an
obstinate struggle the greater half of Europe,
extirpating Protestantism in Italy and in France,
in Belgium and in South Germany, in Bohemia
and Austria, literature and philosophy underwent
the same influence. At the very moment when
Italy lost the monopoly of Fine Arts, and high
schools of painting rose in Madrid, Seville, and the
Spanish Netherlands, a new poetry and a new
poetical style began to spread from Spain all over

Europe. Not only Italian and German Marinists were imitators of the Spanish Gongorists, even your English Euphuism of Shakspeare's times had its origin in the *culteranismo* of Spain; and not the form and style alone, but the spirit also, and the subjects of literature during the first half of the seventeenth century, were in the main Spanish. Only think of Corneille's ' Cid,' written in 1636, of his ' Polyeucte,' which might figure among Calderon's *Autos sagramentales*. Even in the second half of the century, Molière takes the subjects of his 'Festin de Pierre,' his 'Princesse d'Elide,' his ' Ecole de Maris,' from Moreto and Tirso. Grimmelshausen introduces into Germany, Scarron into France, the Roman *picaresco* of the Spaniards, of which Lesage and Smollett became the recognised masters in the following century. Much greater still is the influence exercised by Spain on the philosophical thought of Europe during the seventeenth century. The death of individuality which accompanied or followed the Spanish rule in State, Church and School, wherever it reached, threatened even speculative activity. Not that the philosophy of Molina and Suarez—if one may call philosophy what after all was only theology ever really penetrated into the higher strata of intellectual life, even the *élite* of the clergy protesting against it, as they did in our days against the dogma of infallibility; but the principle of authority which Spain had restored all over the world was a powerful check on continental thought, a check sometimes beneficial, more often most pernicious. There can be no doubt that no society could live in the long run with the principles, or rather the absence of principles, of the Italian Renaissance. The restoration of authority was the imposition of a salutary rein on daring minds for whom the *licet quia libet* had become a species of dogma. However, if you think how Malebranche, and even Descartes, were fettered in the movement of their thought by the reigning dogmatism of their time, you may well ask yourselves whether the benefit was not bought too dear. *Je trouve bon qu'on n'approfondisse pas l'opinion de Copernic*, says the great enemy of the Jesuits himself. It was because Catholic Europe did not dare to grapple with this *opinion* that the leadership of modern thought passed from it to the Protestant countries of England and Holland, where there was no Holy Inquisition to interrupt the researches of a Galileo, no unbending orthodoxy to stop the mighty thought of a Pascal.

The Reformation had been a popular movement, not an aristocratical one, as scientific Protestant-activity must be everywhere and always. The great Protestant men of science of the preceding century, the Reuchlin and Erasmus, the Henry Estienne and Justus Scaliger, were sons of the Italian Renaissance, not of the German Reformation. Their inspiration was a thoroughly worldly one, they acted upon the aristocracy of culture, not on the masses. The Reformation sprung more from a moral feeling of revolt, than from an intellectual want of liberty. This is the reason why I scarcely mention it here, where I look only for the formation of European thought, as it manifests itself in the higher sphere of select intelligence. For, whatever may be the character of moral life, in intellectual life the *paucis vivit genus humanum* will always remain a truth. If, however, the Reformation was not a philosophical movement in its origin, it had the most momentous influence on the philosophical movement by its consequences. Modern Catholicism, indeed, such as it was shaped by the Jesuits during the sixteenth century, if it did not combat openly the classical civilisation and literature which the Renaissance had uncovered, as it were, and given back to humanity, yet knew how to paralyse its action in the most effective way. Nowhere was the Greek and Latin literature more industriously studied than in the Jesuit schools ; but it was previously rendered innocuous. The poison of free thought which it contains was taken out of it, before it was served to the youthful mind. The freest and most living of all literatures became a collection of dead rhetorical formulæ to be learnt by heart and to be used as occasion demanded. The matter was represented as of no value whatever; the form only as a charming and clever play of the mind. Just so three centuries later, when it was no longer possible to ignore the development of natural sciences, the Jesuits reduced all the results of long and universal research into manuals to be used and mechanically applied in practical life, or to be confided to memory for examination's sake, where it answers so well, indeed, that the *rue des Postes* drills ten times more successful scholars for the *école polytechnique* than any lay establishment, although history does not say that it has produced one man of science. For they are prudent enough to teach the scientific data without awakening and stimulating that spirit of research which is the ideal

value of natural science, as freedom of thought is
the true ideal value of ancient literature. Not so
Protestantism.   That also had restored authority
in place of the theory of unlimited liberty which
in the times of Italian Renaissance made caprice
the supreme arbiter of life.   But its authority
was not an outward one; it was the authority
of individual conscience.   Its main principle
was free inquiry, first applied to the Bible ;
but once allowed to exercise itself, there was no
telling where it would stop, and in fact, it did *not*
stop at the Bible.

It was not the cradle of Protestantism, however, which first saw these fruits of the new faith.
German Protestantism was temporarily quenched,
when the reaction against Spanish dogmatism set
in in Europe ; and poor Kepler was almost stifled
in his attempts to develope the system of
Copernicus.   Germany was engaged in the most
disastrous and barbarous war that the history of
mankind mentions in its annals, when the noble
scientific movement of the seventeenth century
England   was in its full vigour. It was reserved
1600-1700.   to England whose great Queen had saved
for her the treasure of religious independence, to
give the signal of the new march onward ; while

Holland, which had come out victorious from the long and manly struggle against Catholic Spain, associated herself with England in the glorious task.

This self-given task was the knowledge of nature and its laws. The fifteenth century had, as it were, restored the broken links of time; the seventeenth unveiled space. The former had shown to man his place in history, the latter was to assign him his place in nature. The world was weary of rhetoric and words, as well as of abstract, bottomless speculation. It thirsted for facts. It had long enough accepted *bonâ fide* the ready-made solutions of all questions offered to it by authority; it was resolved to inquire for itself into the causes of things. The conclusions of an *à priori* philosophy would no longer satisfy it. Secretly and almost unconsciously it longed for a knowledge based on observation, which should also be a methodical knowledge. It was Bacon who gave words to the innermost desire of his generation, when he introduced and recommended the method of induction. No doubt, Copernicus had observed before him and better than he did. Kepler was just then practising 'induction,' from observations with

positive results, of which Bacon could not boast,
whilst Galileo was at the same moment employing
the experimental method which Bacon still used
very awkwardly. Nevertheless it is Bacon, not
Kepler or Galileo, who is rightly considered the
father of modern thought. Kepler and Galileo
indeed used the inductive and experimental
method somewhat as M. Jourdain made prose—
sans le savoir. Assuredly the progress of science
was not the less furthered because Galileo's grand
and simple nature, and Kepler's noble and unbending mind, were occupied with the search for truth
without being aware of the intellectual revolution
they helped to bring about. Nevertheless, for the
history of thought, the man who first spoke out
and formulated the new method with the full
consciousness of the momentous principle he
expressed, remains the representative man of the
age. It is the fashion nowadays, on the continent
at least, to look down upon Bacon, because he was
an indifferent observer and a sometimes puerile
experimentalist; a little also because he was a fine
writer, and our time happens to be in a somewhat
suspicious disposition of mind towards fine language. It is only just, however, to remember
that Bacon's whole education still belonged to the

rhetorical period; that his very nature was of an
artistic turn; and, above all, that, if he did not
do much to further science by his discoveries,
he advanced it immensely by the impulse which
he gave to it by establishing the new method.
Once might say that from that time only, the
ground was won on which methodical empiricism
could move freely.   Not only did Hobbes take his
start from Bacon; but all that England discovered in natural philosophy from Harvey to
Newton, all that it produced in psychological
philosophy from Locke to Hume, would have been
impossible, if the *Novum Organon* had not laid
down the laws of the exact method.

It would have been equally impossible if the
Protestant faith had not been maintained in
England during that time.   The melancholy lot
of Kepler, G. Bruno, and Galileo, would have been
reserved for these daring hunters for truth, if they
had not lived on Protestant ground.   The three
greatest continental thinkers of the mathematical
age—Descartes, Spinosa, Leibnitz—could perform
their work only because they passed the greater
part of their lives in Protestant countries.   One
of them carried even there the invisible fetters
imposed upon him by his first education.   Nay,

c 2

Bayle himself, who forms the link between the
seventeenth and eighteenth centuries, between
English and French thought, was obliged to invoke the protection of the Protestant governments
of the Hague and London.

If English Empiricism [1] was a reaction against
Spanish Dogmatism ; if Spanish Dogmatism had
been a reaction against Italian Humanism,
French Rationalism, which ruled supreme during the following century,
was a continuation of, not an opposition to,
the intellectual current in England.   It was a sort
of contagion, indeed, which affected France, whose
most distinguished geniuses, from Saint-Evremond
to Montesquieu, from Voltaire to Buffon, and even
down to Rousseau, came in turn to England, and
even before crossing the Channel had put themselves to the school of Newton and Locke.   No
sooner had France taken the lead than she gave
to the movement that particular logical character
of her own, which goes straight to the mark and
never shrinks from the last conclusions.   The
great English thinkers of the preceding age con-

*France,
1770–1775.*

---

[1] By Empiricism I mean the spirit of the seventeenth century, *i.e.* the mechanical and mathematical explanation of
Nature, as it was undertaken and to a great extent carried out.

tented themselves with studying things and facts
without trying to draw from them inferences which
might be too dangerous, or applying them to
religion and politics.   Locke himself paused in
deep reverence before revelation and the throne.
Not so the French.   Their rationalistic turn of
mind and impatient temperament carried them
at once to the extreme of submitting church
and state to the same method of inquiry which
had been so successfully applied to nature and
mind.   But logic and passion soon drove them
further than they first intended, and made them
often forget that patient observation and careful
comparison of facts, which had yielded such
extraordinary results in England.   Already Descartes—a true Frenchman in that respect—had at
once committed himself to the mechanical explanation of things, by making the animal a
machine, and as he remained a spiritualist at
heart, never could quite manage to reconcile the
two worlds of matter and mind.   The French of
Bayle's school—I do not say Bayle himself—knew
of no such impediments.   They recognised no
authority whatever.   Their aim was simply absolute emancipation from all conventionality and
authority.   Without being aware of it, they fell

again into the authoritative spirit, against which
the English reaction was directed. Only it was
no longer revelation, nor tradition which was the
authority, but the senses and human reason, —
human reason independent, if not of natural, at
least of historical facts. They dreamed either of
political constitutions (which were to be the result
not of history, *i.e.* of conflicting interests, but
of a general, abstract, preconceived idea of state
and society) ; or of a natural law, which was to
replace the codes of traditional laws and customs,
just as they dreamed of a natural, or rather a
rational, religion, which began with being a timid
deism, very similar to that of Toland and Clarke,
and ended with the enthronement of the goddess
of reason, or with the complete denial of that
spiritual world, from which Descartes had
been unable to throw a bridge to the world
of matter.

Whatever may have been the fatal consequences of this method for France herself, though
they are largely balanced by its salutary results,
the method itself effected the liberation of Europe,
nay of mankind. There existed an accumulation of traditional forms, prejudices, impediments
of all sorts which disturbed the development of

humanity. It seems to have been the historical mission of France, it certainly was her merit, a merit which never can be sufficiently acknowledged, to have laid the axe unsparingly to this thicket of intellectual conventionalities, and levelled the road for us. Of course she could not remove all—it was not desirable that she should remove all; and much of the brushwood which she removed, has grown up again. Still it was the first time in history that men dared to look at things and to order them by the light of reason alone. Many national qualities had singled France out for this task, many circumstances helped her to fulfil her mission with immediate success. The clearness of the French mind, as it reveals itself in the French language; the geographical position of the country between England, Spain, and Germany; the political hegemony over Europe which she had won under Louis XIV.; the vast influence gained already by her poetical literature; last, not least, the simplicity of the new creed, based upon the most general characteristics of humanity and common-sense, and carried out by the most seductive of instruments, logic—all contributed to facilitate her task.

This explains also the instantaneousness with

which the French idea made its way in Europe.
Generally, the intellectual influence of a nation
only begins to spread abroad when its work is nearly
completed. Italy had already done her best, when
towards the beginning of the sixteenth century
her thoughts and works began to act upon the
rest of Europe. For more than a century Europe
still continued to go to Rome, Bologna, and Naples,
although Velasquez and Murillo, Poussin and
Claude, Rubens and Van Dyck, were capable of
teaching their teachers. It was the same with
Spain and England. It is the same with Germany, whose original and creative work was done
and well-nigh finished as early as 1850, although
the world is looking upon her still as the great
laboratory of thought for Europe. France is,
perhaps, the only country which began to export
her intellectual wares at once, even before the
whole store was gathered and ready. The time of
Voltaire and the Encyclopædists was also the time
of Hume and Gibbon.

It was reserved for Germany to react against
the too absolute thought of France, and to begin
Germany, 1760–1825. the work of restoration on a sounder
basis than that which Spain had tried to
lay two centuries before. It would be interesting

to show, at some length, how she prepared herself for her task, how she fulfilled it, and what were the results obtained from it. To do this properly, however, it would be necessary to prove how she owed part, at least, of her intellectual freedom to England and France, how from them she certainly received the impulse to her own work, how she renovated philosophy as well as history, how she created several new sciences which have since taken their place amongst the greatest achievements of the human mind. Suffice it to state that she introduced once for all the idea of *Organism* into European thought, just as French Rationalism, English Empiricism, Spanish Dogmatism, and Italian Humanism, have long become integral parts of the mental constitution of Europe. Is it not in fact as impossible now for us to read Homer in the same spirit in which our grandfathers read him before Wolf had written his ' Prolegomena,' as it is for us to look at Nature as we might have done before Newton had published his ' Principia,' or at the State as we might have done before Montesquieu wrote his ' Esprit des Lois ' ?

There is, indeed, a common stock of ideas on which we all live, in which we all move, often

without being quite conscious of it. Let even
the most convinced of Roman Catholics ask himself whether he could still look on the history of
mankind as St. Thomas or St. Dominic looked on
it before the Italian Renaissance had restored, as
it were, the continuity of history, and filled up the
abyss which cut humanity in two. Could any
man consider public and private life with the
unprincipled *naïveté* with which the contemporaries
of Machiavelli considered them, before the principle of authority had been restored by Spain?
Again, who of us could ever forget, for a moment
only, the physical discoveries of the seventeenth
century, and think of the earth, like Dante, as
the centre of creation? And is it not the same
with our political and philosophical views? Has
not the application of the French rationalistic
method of the past century moulded our mind
anew? Could we still, if we wished, look on the
divine right of monarchy or on revelation as
Bossuet and Fénelon did? Now something
analogous has taken place since the death of Voltaire and Rousseau. Another new thought has
become an integral part of the European mind.
It would be as impossible for Hume to write
his essay on 'National Character' to-day as

it would have been for Augustin Thierry to write his 'Conquête d'Angleterre' in the past century, or for anyone to compose Voltaire's 'Pucelle' in ours. Why so? Because not only have there been discoveries in philology and ethnography which render it materially impossible to explain historical facts as a Hume or Gibbon explained them, but also because a new idea has been thrown into the world, which has profoundly modified our whole course of thought. Now this idea has been elaborated in Germany, and it is the history of this elaboration which is still to be written, and of which I venture to offer something like a general programme, the outlines of a plan, which it would require volumes to fill in.

In speaking of the intellectual movement of Germany, from the second half of the past century to the middle of the present, it will be in-dispensable also to touch upon her poeti-cal literature and her philosophy proper. Definition of the subject.
This seems to be a sort of truism. Yet it is not so in my mind. What I am investigating now is neither the literary spirit, nor the meta-physical speculations, nor the scientific work of the nation, but the whole *Weltanschauung*, that is

to say, the general course of thought (or rather
the general standing-point), which the German
nation made for itself, and opened or added to
European culture during those seventy or eighty
years; and such a general standing-point is but
indirectly influenced by poetry and science proper.
Poetry is an art, and as such it is not subject to
the law of progress; consequently it is, properly
speaking, outside history, a thing absolute and
eternal. The 'Iliad' is as true to-day as it was
three thousand years ago, the main object of poetry
being the unchangeable part of man's nature. It
is not so with science, with thought, with politics.
These are subject to the law of development.
When we read in Dante's poem of Francesca's love
and Pia's death we are moved as Dante's contemporaries may have been moved; when he explains
his cosmography to us, we smile, and perhaps
shut *il suo volume*. Here, then, we speak of two
different activities of the human mind, which
sometimes are at work in a different, sometimes
in the same, generation and country. England's philosophical labour began only after
Shakespeare, that of France only after Racine
and Molière; whereas in Spain Calderon and Cervantes were the contemporaries of Suarez and

Molina, while in Germany Goethe and Schiller lived at the same time with Kant and Wolf, Humboldt and Niebuhr. This apparently accidental fact has an important consequence. Poetry and philosophy penetrate each other, when they are simultaneous, to their mutual advantage in some respects, to their great disadvantage in others. The spirit of Calderon's poetry is also the spirit of Ignatius Loyola ; in Schiller you hear the echo of Kant's moral philosophy. The great literature of the French, on the contrary—the eloquence of a Bossuet and the enthusiasm of a Corneille— expresses a state of thought in some points directly opposed to that spirit of the eighteenth century which the world calls properly the French spirit. I might speak of Shakespeare, for whose clear, deep eye there is no yesterday nor to-morrow, no here nor there, without even mentioning that he was a contemporary of Bacon ; I could not speak of Goethe without reminding you that he was a friend of Herder, and a reader of W. von Humboldt.

There is another fact of great importance which I could not pass over in silence if I had space to enter fully into the subject ; and this is the political state of Germany during the elabora-

tion of her Thought (*Weltanschauung*), and the
effect which this thought has had on the ulterior
transformation of the German State.   This great
period during which the intellectual culture of
Germany was built up or at least accomplished,
was the time when her old society was dissolved,
and her political life was in complete decay.   Is
it possible to be at the same time great and fertile
in public life, and in scientific and speculative
activity ?   When we think of Plato and Aristotle
laying the foundation of all true and high philosophy in the period of decay which had followed
the epoch of what might be called the civil war of
Greece; when we contemplate the political disunion and misery of Italy at the time of the
Renaissance ; when we see England contribute
most actively to the intellectual wealth of Europe
during the not very glorious reigns of James I. and
Charles II.; when we observe France ruling the
world by the pen of Voltaire and Rousseau, sending
the missionaries of her thought to St. Petersburg
and Naples, to Copenhagen and Lisbon, and at the
same time defeated at Rossbach, obliged to sign the
peace of Aix-la-Chapelle and that of Versailles, and
driven out from India and her colonies ; when we
think of Germany producing her Kant and Herder,

while the Fatherland was utterly impotent and
helpless, or even under foreign domination, we
may be tempted to think that perhaps the two
activities are incompatible, or at least only excep-
tionally compatible.

And why should it be otherwise? Must not
the different faculties of the human mind have
their rest from time to time and relieve each
other, if the sources are not to be exhausted before
the time? There have been religious ages, like
the first centuries of our era and the sixteenth
century, entirely bent upon the creation and
definition of religious dogmas, passionate only
for religious questions and interests; and these
have been followed by periods of comparative
silence, when humanity, weary of theological discussions, uninterested in religious subjects,
quietly accepted the existing forms of religion and
rested in them. There had been a great artistic
age four centuries before Christ, slowly prepared
during hundreds of years, slowly dying out during
hundreds of years, after a short and brilliant
blossom. Then the capacity of artistic intuition lay dormant for a long, long time, till
it slowly awakened towards the end of the
Middle Ages, and came to a short but splendid

efflorescence in the fifteenth century only again
to die a long death, which, I am afraid, is now well
nigh consummated.   But here again I must warn
my hearers against taking my words too literally.
There have been eminent statesmen like Richelieu
in scientific ages, religious apostles like Savonarola
in artistic centuries ; so there may be eminent ✱
artists in our time—but they act as isolated individuals.   The main effort of the human mind is
bent in another direction, and there are but few
eyes open to take in what is still left of artistic
creation.

Why should not the capacity for political and
scientific life sometimes lie fallow, when the religious and artistic faculties require such temporary
repose ?   Why should they not have their rest
in turn ?   Why, above all, should we discuss
which grandeur is the better, that of Voltaire or
that of Napoleon, that of Newton or that of
Cromwell ?   Men will never agree on that question,
because it is not a difference of opinion, but a
difference of temperament and character.   Let us
only admit this one point.   When a nation, in-
stinctively or consciously, feels that one day's work
is done and sets herself to do the work of the next,
leave her alone ; do not let us try to be wiser than

history and nature. If for a time a nation gives herself up to building, laboriously and awkwardly perhaps, a new house in which she may live unmolested and in conformity with her own history and nature, let her do so, and do not ask of manhood the down of youth, nor of summer the mellow tints and ripe fruits of autumn. All these are at the bottom idle questions, which are much like reproaching the apple-tree for not bearing oranges. If the nation which has yielded the intellectual leadership of Europe to another nation, because it had more pressing work on hand—perhaps also because it was tired and wanted change—excludes itself from the intellectual life of Europe, as Spain did during the seventeenth and eighteenth centuries, it will pay a penalty heavy enough. If, on the contrary, it continues to participate in the spiritual movement of Europe, as this country has done during the eighteenth and nineteenth centuries, then it may be sure that one day or another the leadership will come back to it, and that sooner or later, it will reoccupy, even if it be only for a time, the first place in the intellectual laboratory of Europe.

However this may be, the assigned limits of time force me to resist the temptation of giving

D

even a sketch of German literature and philosophy proper, still more of relating the history of state and religion in Germany, and I must content myself with simply tracing the outlines and the general character of German culture, such as it was shaped in the period I have mentioned. Even thus I shall be obliged to have recourse to somewhat superficial generalities in explaining the growth and the nature of the German standing-point in religion, literature, politics, and science. I need scarcely add that my remarks have not the slightest pretension to originality. I give you the results neither of special investigation, nor of personal thought; but only what is the common property of every cultivated German, although I give it in the particular form which it has taken by passing through my individual mind. I speak only as an interpreter, not even as a commentator, still less as a critic, and least of all as a discoverer of new truth.

One word more and I have finished. A subject like the one which we propose to study, the contribution of one European nation to the common capital of European thought, can only be successfully treated if we endeavour to divest ourselves of all party spirit, national, political, and religious. Party spirit has its right place in practical life. When it is a question of defending one's faith, or one's country, of obtaining certain positive ends only to be obtained by collective and disciplined forces, let us be of a party and stand by it *usque ad mortem*. But when we try to understand the history of mankind and to penetrate its mysterious ways, nay, whenever we meet on a ground where those practical interests are not endangered or threatened, where there is no war and strife, where we are simply to live with each other, to know each other, at the utmost to judge each other—let us forget such unpleasant distinctions, and treat each other as if we were all of one nation, one party, one faith. Let us not approach peoples, or facts, or ideas with a preconceived judgment, nor ask them suspiciously for their passport, instead of trying to ascertain their intrinsic value. Let us not condemn or canonize people, facts or ideas, because they may be of Russian or Italian origin, bear a Catholic or Protestant label, come from the Conservative or Liberal camp. This would be true barbarism,—barbarism, I am afraid, which will invade humanity more and more, in proportion as political democracy advances with superficial enlightenment

and scientific half-culture. As the number of
those who take part in public life increases, the
more will passion—political, religious, national—
overrule justice and equity and goodwill. For
the man who puts himself under the thraldom of
party bonds must needs sacrifice part of the truth
which he knows, part of his moral and intellectual
freedom, part of himself. On the other side, in
proportion to the scantiness of their numbers will
be the intensity of the love of truth in those who
emancipate themselves from such passions in order
to look at things and judge them by themselves.
Let us all strive at least to be of those few; for
they are not only the lovers of truth, they are not
only the sole free minds, they alone are also the
really just. And whatever our effeminate age
may say to the contrary, justice is still and will
always be what Plato and Aristotle proclaimed it
to be, the highest and manliest of virtues.

LECTURE II.

NOBODY can form a true estimate of the present
state of Germany, social and political, religious
and intellectual, who does not realise what was
her starting-point.   All European nations can
boast of a continuous development from the Middle
Ages to the nineteenth century.   Even the great
catastrophe which delivered Italy up to foreign rule
towards the middle of the sixteenth century, even
the Great Rebellion and the Glorious Revolution
which gave birth to new England, nay, even the
revolution of 1789 which destroyed the *ancien
régime* in France, had not the power entirely to
break the thread of national history in these three
great civilised nations.   From Dante and Giotto to

Filijaca and Dominichino there is one uninterrupted
line of growth and decay.   The memory of Queen
Bess was still living in the time of William III., and
a Lamartine and a Victor Hugo have been lulled
with the verse of Lafontaine and Racine, and
reared on the ideas of Bossuet and Voltaire.   Not
so in Germany.   The Thirty Years' War which
raged from 1618 to 1648 made a gap in her
national development, such as we find nowhere
else in history.   It threw her back full two
hundred years, materially and intellectually, and
extinguished all remembrance of the past.

If you walk through the cities of Augsburg and
Nüremberg, Lübeck and Ratisbon, you meet at

Germany
in the six-
teenth
century.

every step vestiges of a high civilisation.
Those churches, those town-halls, those
palaces—only think of the Heidelberg-
Schloss—were mostly built at the end of the sixteenth or the beginning of the seventeenth century;
and a hundred and fifty years before, Æneas
Sylvius (Pope Pius II.) had been so struck with
the comfort of the German cities, that he declared
the kings of Scotland might rejoice to be as well-
housed as an ordinary burgher of Nüremberg.
True, the relative poverty of the soil always rendered the accumulation of wealth difficult and

slower than elsewhere in two-thirds of Germany; true also, the discovery of America and the consequent change of the seat of commerce had in some measure checked the tide of German middle-class prosperity. Nevertheless the material and social civilisation of Germany was still in the sixteenth century on the whole rather superior than inferior to that of England and France. If we think of the high culture of city patricians like Pirckheimer and Peutinger, of bankers like Fugger and Welser, of lords and gentlemen like Philip of Hesse and Ulrich von Hutten; if we think of their intimacy with artists such as Vischer and Dürer, with scholars such as Reuchlin and Erasmus, with theologians such as Luther and Melanchthon, we at once feel that there exists an intellectual culture common to the whole nation, that wealth is not yet separated from learning, that Art is not yet the métier of a guild. Not only English and French courtiers, but also the highly refined Italians, who crossed the Alps, found in Germany a society quite on a par with that of Florence and Ferrara. True it is that politically, and even intellectually, the country made little progress after the religious peace of 1555. Ever since a foreigner, Charles V., had ascended the

imperial throne in 1519, the German national
state seemed doomed to death, and all patriotic
minds felt it deeply.   All towards the end of the
century looked with eyes of melancholy envy
on the national kingdoms of Queen Elizabeth
and Henry IV.   But this is not the place to relate
the history of the sixteenth history.   Suffice it to say
that the political unity of Germany had declined
more and more, that the Jesuits had won consider-
able ground, not only over the Lutherans, but also
over the National Catholics, as we might call all
the representatives of the old religion, who in
Germany as in France resisted the new cosmopolitan current of the Church.   The whole of the
second half of the century was employed in that
double work of reaction, political and religious,
and the work was successful.

Still there remained the tradition of a German
state, there remained some public life, there re-
Germany   mained above all a good deal of the
in the
seventeenth German religion.   All this Ferdinand II.
century.   undertook to destroy, and, although he
was conquered in the long run, he succeeded only
too well.   Germany came out of the Thirty Years'
War almost expiring.   It was as if a deadly illness
had wiped out the memory of the nation in its

cruel delirium. All the national forces, material as well as intellectual and moral, were destroyed when peace was concluded in 1618. There are fertile wars and sterile wars ; civil and religious wars belong mostly to the latter class. Still the religious wars in France, and the Great Rebellion in England, were light spring storms compared with that terrible Thirty Years' War which left Germany a desert. And what it destroyed in this way was not a barbarous country ; it was an old civilisation. Hundreds of Material flourishing cities were reduced to ashes ; state. there were towns of 18,000 inhabitants which counted but 324 at the peace ; ground which had been tilled and ploughed for ten centuries had become a wilderness; thousands of villages had disappeared. Trees grew in the abandoned houses. At Wiesbaden the market had grown into a brush-wood full of deer. The whole Palatinate had but 200 freeholders; Würtemberg had but 48,000 inhabitants at the end of the war instead of the 400,000 which it had mustered at the beginning. We are told that a messenger going from Dresden to Berlin through a once flourishing country walked thirty miles without finding a house to rest in. The war had devoured, on an average, three quarters of

the population, two thirds of the houses, nine
tenths of the cattle of all sorts; nearly three
quarters of the soil had been turned into heath.
Commerce and industry were as utterly destroyed
as agriculture; the mighty Hanseatic League was
dissolved; the savings of the nation were entirely
spent. I am therefore certainly not far from the
truth when I say that Germany was thrown back
two hundred years as compared with Holland,
France, and England. Even in so prolific a nation,
a century did not suffice to fill up the gaps in the
population, nor could two centuries restore the lost
capital. It is a proved fact, indeed, that Germany
recovered only towards 1850 the actual amount of
capital and the material well-being with which she
had entered the great war in 1618. Thus, so
far as the number of homesteads, the heads
of cattle, the returns of crops can be statistically
ascertained, the amount in 1850 was, not relatively
but absolutely, the same as in 1618; in some
respects even inferior.

The social and moral state corresponded
with the material. Many schools and churches
Moral and stood abandoned, for public instruction
social state. and public worship had nearly perished.
The highly cultivated language of Luther was

utterly forgotten, together with the whole literature of his time. The most vulgar vices had
taken root in people who had been reared from
their infancy in the horrors of war. Every higher
aim and interest had been lost sight of; not
a vestige of a national tradition remained.
There was no middle class nor gentry left; the
higher noblemen had become petty despotic
princes, with no hand over them, since the
Emperor was but a name; the lower went to their
court to do lackey's service. A whole generation
had grown up during the war, and considered its
savage barbarism as a normal state of society.
Only those who have read the 'Simplicissimus,' an
admirable novel in Smollett's style, but anterior
·by more than a century, can have an idea of
the state of things. Suicides became so frequent
after the war, that an Imperial law ordered
self-murderers to be buried under the gallows.
From houses and churches the old artistic furniture
had disappeared, and was replaced by coarse
and cheap utensils. The peasants' dwellings
differed little from those of their animals. De-
preciation of their products and taxation weighed
heavily upon them; the innumerable differences
of weight and money, and the bad roads rendered ·

the sale of goods more difficult still. The administration of justice was detestable, slow, expensive,
and corrupt. For all habits of self-government,
even in the cities, had gone; the gentlemen
had become courtiers instead of magistrates. An
unprecedented coarseness of manners had invaded
not only courts and cities, but also the universities
and the clergy. There was servility everywhere.
The theologians became in theory and practice
the supporters of despotism; a Leibnitz himself
at times set a somewhat unworthy example of
humility. Cowardice had become the common vice
of the lower people and of what remained of the
middle class, in a time when the free citizens were
weaned from the use of arms through the numerous
mercenary troops, which had become gangs of
highwaymen. The prodigality, vanity, and luxury
of the higher classes infected the lower; the contagion was general. Everybody wanted a title—
for it was then that the great title-mania set in,
of which Germany is not yet entirely cured. Theology in its most rigid form, superstition of the
rudest character, had replaced religion; pedantry
had taken the place of erudition. The study of
the Greek language had almost disappeared from
the universities and colleges, where the professors

vied with the students in vulgar vices. Drinking became a profession; there were travelling
drinkers; at the highest Court of the Empire at
Wetzlar, an examination in drinking was exacted
from the newly-appointed assessors by their col-
leagues. Every baron had his mistresses, as
well as an Augustus of Saxony, or a George of
Hanover. 'At the Court of Dresden,' says a contemporary, ' there are numbers of people who, not
being able to live from their own resources, sacrifice their wives to maintain themselves in favour.'
Gambling had become a general habit, and as
nobody had money to gamble with, it was the
public income which, through the channel of the
princes, ran into the pockets of the courtiers and
became the means of satisfying that passion.
Venality and nepotism prevailed among the numerous officials; pauperism and mendicity among the
lower people; ignorance and immorality everywhere. The nobility and bourgeoisie, once so
united, were henceforth separated, it seemed, for
ever. Foreign manners and foreign language
were adopted everywhere. Read the letters of the
Duchess of Orleans, read Lady M. Montague's
reports of the beginning of the following century,
or Pöllnitz's and Casanova's memoirs, in order to

form for yourselves an idea of the prevalent customs
and language. The restoration of the Stuarts,
and the splendour of the French court, acted as
dangerous examples; every princeling wanted to
imitate them. 'There is not a younger son of a
side line,' said Frederick II., even a century later,
'who does not imagine himself to be something
like Louis XIV. He builds his Versailles, has his
mistresses, and maintains his armies.' Now this
splendour, without glory and taste, without refinement and art, without literature, without any
redeeming point, in short, became general at
the hundreds of German courts, and did not allow
the exhausted country to rally. Never, perhaps,
were things worse than towards 1700, when the
court poet of Dresden, Besser, sang his well-known
ode :

> Der König ist vergnügt;
> Das Land erfreuet sich.[1]

The political state was not better than the
social. Ferdinand II. had not succeeded in his
Political plans; he was conquered. The States
state. became free; religion also was free; but
one-third of Germany was virtually separated and

---

[1] The king amuses himself : the country is delighted.

estranged from the intellectual life of the nation.
Austria and Bavaria have only in this century
begun again to take a part in it. All the wealthy,
the learned, the industrious, who would not give
up their faith, were exiled like Kepler; those
who remained were broken in spirit. National
unity scarcely existed even in words and forms.
The Empire was organised anarchy : *confusio
divinitus conservata*, said Oxenstierna. Germany
had really and truly become a geographical expression. France and Austria governed her in
turn; the Germans themselves saw in Louis XIV.
the successor of Charlemagne, called to protect
them against Spaniards and Turks. The small
states, which the court-theologians called com-
placently 'true gardens of God, cultivated by
princely hands,' had in reality become hot-beds of
debauch and tyranny. Never had despotism
reigned so supreme and unchecked. And what
despotism ! Not that of a Philip II. or a Louis
XIV., which at least pursued high, if unjust,
aims, and exercised itself in grand proportions;
but despotism of the meanest as well as the
pettiest kind. In the interest of their faith
men had stood by the Princes against the
Emperor; now the clergy had become instruments

of the former against the people, preaching everywhere the doctrine of passive obedience to the
' monarchs,' as they styled themselves. The
' monarchs ' in turn isolated themselves more and
more from the nation, which they governed through
the thousands of their servile and corrupt officials,
whose business it was to find the money for their
princely entertainments. Justice was as venal as
administration was rapacious. The old parlia-
ments had disappeared long ago, together with
the jury, the *Landesgemeinde,* and all that recalled
the old Teutonic uses and customs which, fortu-
nately for you, survived in this island. Religion
itself, which had been the pretext of the war, had
well-nigh vanished. True, the nation, in the misery
of her political life, had thrown herself entirely
into Church life, but a Church life of the narrowest
kind, in which theology triumphed over religious
feeling, as it had triumphed over science; for
science and theology again stood apart, as in the
days of scholasticism. And as religion had united
the classes, so theology separated them. Meanwhile Catholic proselytism pursued its work, and
princely conversions became of every-day occurrence.

It is easy from this to infer the intellectual

state of the nation. Here also a gulf had opened
between the learned and the people, as in Intellectual state.
religion between the clergy and the lay-
men. The German literature of the sixteenth
century, the poetry and prose of a Hans Sachs, a
Fischart, a Sebastian Brant, had been essentially
popular. A hundred years later there was as_ complete a separation between literature and the people
as there was complete oblivion of what had existed
before. There was no theatre, and no art; for
art did not survive the war. What remained of
it was of the worst taste, more *bric-à-brac* than art.
It was at this time that the taste for collecting
curiosities arose : the *grüne Gewölbe* in Dresden
dates from this period. In poetry there is the
same utter want of originality. The whole literature of the time is a servile imitation of the Neo-
Latin literatures. Opitz imitates Tasso, Ronsart,
Ben Jonson ; the Silesian school imitates Marini,
Mlle. Scudery, Dryden ; Gottsched and Canitz
imitate Boileau, Racine, Pope. There was nothing national either in the form, the language,
the subjects, or the inspiration. Besides, the writers
were without a public. The bourgeoisie lived
in the narrowest social and intellectual circle.
The gentry were too much given up to 'gambling

E

and drinking,' according to Leibnitz, ' to be lovers
of science like the English, or of wit and witty
conversation like the French.'   The princes, who
might be compared to your lords, 'thought it
beneath their dignity to cultivate their mind.'   So
wrote Count Manntenfel to Wolff as late as 1738.
Leibnitz himself ascribed to his countrymen one
merit only, that of industry.   The language fell into
utter decay ; everybody in the higher classes spoke
French as the Russians did twenty years ago.
' Since the treaty of Münster and the Pyrenees,'
said Leibnitz, ' it is not only the French government, but also the French language which has got
the best of us.   Our princes have rendered Germany subject, if not to the French king—although
there is little wanting for that either—at least to
French fashion and language.'   The official idiom
was composed of Latin, French, and German words
mixed together, and so awkwardly constructed,
that even an English legal document would be
easy reading compared with it.   At the universities teaching went on in Latin.   If there was
still some verse—whatever its worth might be—
there was no prose left in the country of Luther.

Nevertheless *à quelque chose malheur est bon*,
and *ogni male non viene per nuocere*.   However

great may have been the misery, the humiliation
and the dismemberment of Germany, however
radical her material, intellectual and moral ruin ;
there yet remained for the nation at
least the possibility of a moral and political restoration.   But she would have lost

*The work-
ing up,
1648–1768.*

this if she had fallen under the Habsburg yoke,
and if Jesuitism had invaded North and Central
Germany as it invaded Austria and Bavaria,
which were secluded from the intellectual and
moral life of Germany for more than a century
after.   The two springs around which the new life
gathered and grew up were the Prussian State
and the Protestant Religion.

Ever since Esau of Saxony had sold his primo-
geniture for the lentil dish of the Polish crown,
the task of reuniting Protestant Germany
had fallen to Prussia, and she did not

Political.

shrink from her glorious mission.   Scarcely was
the Peace of Westphalia signed when the Great-
Elector set about the task, as a disinterested
servant of the people, and one conscious of his
duty.   Nor was it easy to do for Germany, in the
broad daylight of modern history, what Egbert
had done for England in the dim times of the early
Middle Ages, what Louis XI. and Ferdinand the

Catholic had accomplished for Spain and France in the fifteenth century, when means were still allowed which were no longer tolerated in the times of Cromwell and William III. This task was the unification of a great nation through the union and assimilation, or the submission, of all the minor states. Nor were the seventeenth and eighteenth centuries times in which public men could speak freely. The Continent was everywhere under the sway of absolute monarchy. Absolute monarchy then guided the state with the instruments at its disposal. These were the army, the bureaucracy, the clergy, and the schools. When 'enlightened despotism' set to work, the first thing was to improve and furbish up these instruments, to enforce discipline, industry, honesty, and to awaken the sense of duty. They were rude masters, those kings of Prussia, who rose early, worked hard, went about themselves, stick in hand, to see that the schoolmasters held their classes, that the tax-gatherers kept their accounts rightly, that the contractors made no undue profits, that every judge had clean hands, and that every official was up to his task. When they began to set the example of economy at their courts in a time when extravagance and prodigality seemed to be the necessary virtues of monarchy, they were sneered at of course as undignified misers. When Frederick II. received coldly adventurers like Pöllnitz and Casanova, who were the delight of all the German courts, he was looked on as a sovereign who did not know what *bon ton* was. The nation, however, was not to be deceived, nor were the thinkers of the time. The friends of enlightenment, from Voltaire down to Diderot, and from Hume to Gibbon, had strong absolutist predilections. You all remember Voltaire's delightful tale about Truth and Reason wandering about Europe after their long banishment, and finding everywhere, except in Poland, signs of a hopeful spring brought about by despotic reformers: it is Pombal in Lisbon, Aranda in Madrid, Tanucci in Naples, Ganganelli in Rome, . Peter Leopold in Tuscany, Joseph II. in Vienna, the great Catherine in St. Petersburg, Struensee in Copenhagen, and Gustavus III. in Stockholm. Even in the little capitals of Stuttgart and Darmstadt, Lippe-Detmold and Dessau, they find 'enlightened despots' on a small footing. The one, however, who was the type and model of them all was Frederick.

Not unjustly. Not only was he the only ruler,

who was in full possession of the culture of his

Frederick the Great. time, the one who had penetrated most deeply into the philosophy of the age, the one who proved the most completely disinterested personally; he was also the one who, from the outset, had the clearest conception of the duty which made him the first servant, ' *le premier domestique*,' of the nation. He was twenty-eight years old when he ascended the throne (1740), and wrote to his officials: ' Our intention is that you should not be allowed to enrich yourselves, and to oppress our poor subjects. You must watch over the welfare of the country as much as over our own; for we will not recognise any distinction between our personal advantage and that of the country; you must always have this in view as much as that—and even more. *The advantage of the country should always have the preference over Our personal advantage*, when both do not concur.' And he not only preached in words, he acted up to his precepts. When seventeen years later he thought himself lost against the coalition of Europe, he wrote on the eve of Rossbach to Count Finck: ' If it happen that I should be killed, affairs must take their course without the slightest alteration, and without any

body perceiving that they are in other hands. . .
If I have the ill luck to be taken prisoner by the
enemy, I forbid my subjects to show the slightest
regard for my person, or to attach the least importance to what I may write from my captivity.
If such a thing should happen, *I wish to be sacrificed
to the State;* and everybody shall obey my brother,
who, as well as my ministers and generals, will
answer *on their heads* that neither province nor
ransom shall be offered for me, but the war shall
be continued just as if I had never existed.' And
what he had proclaimed on his accession and
during his glorious reign, he still recommended
on his death-bed and in his will to his successor;
i.e. 'if necessary, the sacrifice of his personal
advantage to the well-being of the country and
the good of the State.' It is this absence of personal ambition, or avarice, or thirst of pleasure,
this complete identification of himself with the
State,—*i.e.* with an impersonal but living ideal,
which forms the moral grandeur of Frederick, whatever may be the means which he and
all his contemporaries, without exception, used
for the attainment of their ends. It is needless
to speak of his intellectual grandeur: his deeds
are too striking to allow of its being contested.

Frederick's attitude towards religious opinion was one of absolute indifference, and the consequence thereof was absolute toleration. He made no attempt to unite the churches as William III. had done, or as his own grandson tried to do. His policy was to let them alone. 'All religions shall be tolerated in my States,' he wrote, 'and the ministers have only one thing to look to, and that is, that none should do any harm to others; for here every one shall be free to seek his salvation after his own mind' (*à sa façon*). He really was the first to emancipate Europe religiously, to create the purely secular State. 'A prince,' said Kant himself, 'who avows it to be his duty not to prescribe anything to men about their religion, but to leave them complete liberty in that respect, who consequently declines even the proud merit of toleration— such a prince is enlightened and deserves to be praised by his contemporaries, and by a grateful posterity, as the one who first emancipated mankind, and left every man free to use his own reason in matters of conscience.' Similarly, as a civil legislator, he realised the dream of his age by putting natural law in the place of traditional law and custom. His Code (the *Landrecht*), in many of its articles,

reads like the 'Rights of Man' of the French
Revolution and the American Constitution. Well
might Mirabeau say, that he was in advance of
his age by a hundred years.

Frederick has often been reproached with
having shown no interest in German literature,
nay, with having expressed something very like
contempt for German intellectual life. This
seems to me very unjust and unintelligent. When
Frederick came of age towards 1730, and again
when, an ardent youth still, and thirsting for intellectual life, he became king, his country offered him
little, and what it offered—Wolff's philosophy—
he certainly embraced with ardour. But naturally
enough he sought his intellectual food chiefly in
the country which produced most of it, and where
literary activity was just then most intense—in
France. Besides, if ' he was a Frenchman by
education, he was a German by nature,' says
Madame de Staël with great shrewdness ; and if he
thought as a Frenchman, I might add, he acted as
a German. There was nothing in the public life of
Germany to inspire a poet or a writer, until by his
deeds he gave a national subject to poetry, and above
all a national inspiration. It is only after the Seven
Years' War—a fertile war, because a necessary one

—that the Germans began to feel themselves a nation again. Goethe in his own life has vividly described the effect of the war on the general marasmus of the time, and Gleim's poems, and Lessing's 'Minna,' remain as witnesses of the direct inspiration which the nation drew from Frederick's exploits. Nay, his indifference to the literary life of his country was perhaps, I might say certainly, a good thing after all. He allowed it to grow naturally, spontaneously, without giving it a direction in an academical or other sense, contenting himself with levelling the ground for it, with making for it a wholesome atmosphere. If Frederick had not ensured absolute liberty of thought to Germany, her literature never would have been what it became, one of the freest of all literatures since the Greek. Well might Schiller sing:

> Kein Augustisch Alter blühte,
> Keines Mediciiers Güte
> Lächelte der deutschen Kunst:
>   *   *   *   *
> Von dem grössten deutschen Sohne,
> Von des grossen Friedrichs Throne
> Ging sie schutzlos, ungeehrt.[1]

---

[1] No Augustan age flourished, the kindness of no Medicis smiled on German Art. From Germany's greatest son, from the throne of the great Frederick, she went unprotected, unhonoured.

But instead of complaining of this indifference,
Germans ought to thank Frederick for it, in
grateful remembrance of Kant's words: 'The age
of enlightenment was the century of Frederick
the Great.' More than that, the time of the
resurrection of the German nation was the time
of Frederick; for it was he who inspired all that
made the nation capable of self-assertion—heroism, national spirit, religious liberty, modern
law; it was he who gave life and strength to the
nucleus which was to become, and deservedly to
become, the German State.

I said, that next to the Prussian State, it was
Protestantism which allowed Germany to raise
herself out of the state of intellectual Protestant-
and moral misery in which the Thirty ism.
Years' War had left her. Undoubtedly it was a
petrified sort of Protestantism which had survived; but it was Protestantism, that is to say,
relative liberty of religious thought. A revival
which assumed the proportions of a new reformation was slowly preparing as early as the second
half of the seventeenth century. This reformation
was not the work of Government, as that Pietism.
of the sixteenth century had been in
England and partly even in Germany. It was

worked out and spread by individuals. So was its
influence an influence on the soul, on the inner
life, not on the constitution of the Church, still less
on government and public life. In both respects,
in its origin and in its effects, it bears a close resemblance to the Evangelical and Wesleyan movement which took place a century later in this
island. It sprang from a want of more intense
religious feeling, and so renovated first religion
and afterwards society. The old theology had forgotten the struggle against sin in the struggle
about dogma; *pietism* left dogma alone, and
appealed to the inner voice of revelation. Pietism,
indeed, which we are so accustomed to look upon
as a narrow or narrowing view of religion, was
at first the exact contrary. It was a reaction
against the dryness and stiffness of orthodox
religion, where theology reigned supreme and
dogmas and forms obstructed the direct and spontaneous communication of the faithful with the
Deity. ' As Socrates, the new apostles said, had
drawn down philosophy from heaven to earth, so
they wished that theology should be turned from
vain speculations and subtleties in order to show
the way of the spirit and of saintliness in the precepts necessary to salvation.' It was thus that

pietism brought warmth, and feeling, and life into
religion, and, although mixed up with mysticism,
acted as a liberating word. This is not the place
to dwell on Spener's and Francke's doings, on
the expulsion of the latter from Leipzig and his
transfer to Halle, which afterwards became the
seat of pietism ; nor can I enumerate the
schools, the charitable institutions, the secularisa-
tion of worship, the collective working establish-
ments which owed their existence to Count Zin-
zendorf and his Herrnhuter (Moravian brethren).
Suffice it to say that the mild charity, the democratic simplicity of these men, won over hundreds
and thousands of souls, and that the movement
which spread from Halle became a general one in
the first half of the past century. Goethe tells
us indeed, 'that 'at this time a certain religious
disposition of mind was rife in Germany. In many
princely houses there was a genuine religious
life ; noblemen were not rare who aimed at true
holiness, and in the lower classes this feeling was
widely spread.' So it came about that pietism grew
into a real power in a very short time. Even the
' monarchs ' began to dread it. The Margrave of
Bayreuth was admonished and rebuked for his
vices by a pietist preacher in presence of the

whole congregation, and publicly promised better
conduct, and all that was required before he could
obtain absolution. When Frederic William I.,
the king-corporal, was dying, his chaplain, a
pietist also, reproached him severely with his
accesses of wrath, his armies, the corvées he had
inflicted on the peasants, and with his failure to do
what he might have done for his poor subjects.

However wholesome and fertile pietism might
be, it was unable to make good the losses which
Scientific   the reformation of the sixteenth century
revival.   had sustained by not bringing about a
political and national reorganisation. This work
was reserved for others. Besides, pietism degenerated but too soon and became in its turn inanimate
and incapable of free action. The inner life,
however, had been awakened, and it was not to
fall asleep again, because those who stopped at
the starting-point claimed the name and inherit-
ance of the initiators. On the other hand the
reigning philosophy was not without influence
on religion; but the reigning philosophy was
not yet that of Locke and Shaftesbury; it was
the theistic philosophy of Descartes, Leibnitz,
and Wolff. The difference is great. The French
and English *amis des lumières* were Deists, that

is to say, they arrived by the application of
the law of causality in the outward world (*i.e.* by
reasoning and mechanical explanation) at the First
Cause or Deity. The German Theists started from
Conscience and tried to prove the Deity by the
inward revelation of the moral law as it speaks in
the bosom of men; and they invoked the authority
of Cartesianism as developed by Leibnitz, and
set forth and commented upon by Wolff, which
appealed to the innate idea of a Deity as the
strongest proof of its existence; whereas Goethe
rightly said of the French of the eighteenth
century what he might also have said of the
English Deists,—'They do not understand that
there can be anything in man which has not come
into him from without.'

The philosophy of Descartes, Leibnitz, and
Wolff influenced science and moral life before it
influenced religion. It was the sight of a superior
foreign literature which first awoke the desire of
a richer intellectual life in Germany. So the admiration of foreign culture became the impulse to
the creation of a national one. For this, however,
it was necessary to emancipate science from
theology, as religion had been emancipated from
it already.

The liberation of man from the yoke of
authority, which was properly *the* idea of the
eighteenth century had been aimed at everywhere
as early as the end of the preceding century, even
in Germany. Whilst Wolff's moral philosophy,
which was only that of Leibnitz in a popularised
form, emancipated morality from theology, it im-
parted also a freer view of legislation. Puffendorf
followed in the footsteps of Hugo Grotius. He drove
the theologians out of political science and founded
a purely lay theory of the state ; and although
individually the German *Lichtfreunde* of that time
were certainly inferior to a Locke and a Bayle, their
immediate practical influence was perhaps greater.
Thomasius not only revolutionised law by his
teaching, putting it on· a natural and rational
basis ; he revolutionised teaching itself by the introduction of the German language into the universities; he founded the German Press by his
weekly papers; he put a stop by his agitation to
that shame of the age, the trials for sorcery and
witchcraft ; he introduced a better tone amongst
professors and students; he dared to say to
Frederick the Great's grandfather that the one
thing wanting for an intellectual and moral
revival in his states was liberty. ' If 1 must say it

in one word,' he wound up his address to King
Frederick, prompting him already to take the lead
of Germany by restoring liberty, ' if I must say it
in one word it is liberty which gives to all spirit
the right life ; and without it human understanding, whatever may be its advantages, is, as it were,
dead and inanimate. . . . This is the one thing
which has given to the Dutch and English so
many learned men, whereas the want of this
liberty has oppressed the inborn sagacity of the
Italians, and the high-flowing mind of the
Spaniards. Such liberty would justify the hope
that in our Germany also noble minds might
apply themselves to wash away that shameful
spot—the belief in her own incapacity to invent
and do anything good and great.' These words
were spoken in 1705.

The University of Halle had been founded
under the protection of the first king of Prussia,
Sophia Charlotte's husband, by the regenerators
of religion, the pietists, who had been persecuted in
Saxony. These, however, had soon fallen themselves into the intolerance from which they had
suffered so much, and waged a terrible war against
Thomasius, to whom the king had offered an
asylum in Halle when he in turn had been driven

F

out of Leipzig. Did he not dare together with
Wolff to preach rationalism in those halls which
the unworthy followers of Spener and Francke considered as their own realm ? Thomasius died
opportunely; Wolff was obliged to leave, when
the persecutors got the better of Frederick I.'s
successor. Then it was that Münchhausen founded
the University of Göttingen, which henceforward
became the stronghold of rationalistic science. It
became also the hearth of that new philology
which paved the way for a freer assimilation of
profane antiquity. Gesner was the first to call the
attention of his pupils to the beauty of ancient
literature, which, till then, had been nothing more
than a drilling instrument; Christ insisted upon
the substance of it, the political, religious, above all
the artistical life of the ancients, and thus became
the creator of modern archæology; whilst Michaelis
through his more methodical study of the eastern
languages, and Heine by his æsthetical commen-
taries, widened the ground and enlivened the
spirit of classical philology.

Meanwhile the material and social life of the
nation began to improve. The process, however, was
very slow, for many of the old hindrances still remained. There was no national centre, no industry,

no commerce. The middle classes might be said to vegetate rather than to live, excluded from all participation in the State, shut up in the petty existence of their small towns, contented in their poverty, and unacquainted with the great currents of life which were flowing elsewhere. Out of their prose of every-day life they fled into the ideal world until they thought that this inner world alone had reality. As soon as the The literary revival. wounds began to heal, the interest in moral and intellectual things was at once re-awakened. First it was religion, soon science and poetry, which became the great affair of the nation, not a pastime for leisure-hours but the one serious thing, not an ornament of life but the national life itself. There were no courts to protect literature, as we have seen, or to guide it. The new literature sprang from the spontaneous activity of the nation. It freed the courts themselves from foreign manners and foreign culture, and forced the national tongue upon them.

Rühmend darf's der Deutsche sagen,
Höher darf das Herz ihm schlagen,
Selbst erschuf er sich den Werth.[1]

[1] The German has a right to boast of it, his heart may beat higher : for he gave to himself his riches.

F 2

There was no return, however, to the popular movement of the sixteenth century, the bridge which might have served for this purpose being irreparably broken. It was a new spirit which rose, individual, not national, but awakening at least, though late, the national spirit, instead of being awakened by it, as was the case elsewhere. Other nations indeed have had a national history and tradition, a centre and a society, wealth and comfort, before they possessed a literature; in Germany it was the reverse. Literature came first, and gave its character to the slowly forming society instead of receiving it from a society already formed. The impulse came from a concourse of isolated and individual forces and efforts which ran into the same bed. There was no political life, or, if there was any, it was beyond the reach of the middle classes; but there arose a literary life, in which there was no division into states and provinces, governed and governing, upper and middle classes. Therein, at least, the nation was one; therein everybody felt himself a German. What a man of talent wrote became at once the property of the nation, whether it was published in Strasburg or in Königsberg, in Frankfort or in Dresden. All the

eminent writers of the age travelled from one end
of the country to the other, and settled where
they pleased. Nobody thought of asking whether
Lessing was a Saxon, Herder a Prussian,
Schiller a Würtemberger. They all formed one
nation. Thus national unity existed in literature
long before its political existence was felt as a
necessity; but it prepared and brought about
political unity in the end. Moreover, and this
specially concerns us here, this literature worked
out an *ensemble* of views which became the lay
creed of every cultivated German, whether Catholic
or Protestant, a creed which is still held by
many, I might say, by the whole *élite*, of
the nation, if not outspokenly, at least as the
tacitly accepted foundation ground of all their
ideas. My object here is to explain what this
creed was.

At the beginning of the eighteenth century
serious attempts had been made to endow
Germany with a national literature; but everything was wanting for original production, form
as well as substance. The language was still,
or rather had become, an unwieldy, awkward
engine, composed of fragments of French, Italian,
Latin, and legal phraseology. There was nothing

in the common life of the nation to furnish
the subject or the matter of a literature; no
original thought, no great action. The consequence was that the new literature continued
to be what the literature of the preceding age
had been—a stammering imitation of French,
Italian, and English models; for Germany had gone
through all the phases through which the western
literatures had passed in the preceding centuries,
following them closely, but without being able to
give any life to its servile copies. Yet the writers
had an instinctive feeling of the task which they
had to fulfil, viz., the creation of a literature at
once popular and refined, national and up to the
mark of western culture. At the same time
they differed as to the way by which this aim
was to be obtained, one side thinking Boileau's
' Art Poétique ' the last word of literary legislation, the others invoking the authority of
English examples. Their appeal, however, was
not made so much to Addison and Pope, rationalists fed with Locke and Shaftesbury, as to
Milton, the poet of enthusiasm, and Richardson the sentimentalist. No doubt they also were
liberal Protestants, but they were not rationalists in the English and French sense of the

word; they were believers, not in the letter
but in the spirit, and even the letter they combated with respect. And this was still the spirit
even of the great literary generation which
followed them, and began to enter the lists
during and shortly after the Seven Years' War
(1756 to 1763).

In the first third of the eighteenth century,
French models still ruled uncontested, and their
advocate, Professor Gottsched, in Leipzig,
was still the absolute sovereign of the Character of the new literature.
German Parnassus. It was against his
pedantic and despotic sway that the so-called
English school arose in Zurich. A whole library
might be filled, not only with the weekly papers,
which for the last twenty years had been trying
awkwardly enough to fill the place of German 'Tat-
lers' and 'Spectators,' but with the heavy volumes
in which the conflicting schools expressed their
theories and attacked those of their adversaries.
Even when an original literature had begun to
spring up, these literary and æsthetical discussions
still continued; in fact, they continued almost to
our day. Modern German literature, you see, was
not born in a simple, spontaneous, unconscious age,
but in an age of criticism; the war of theories

raged over its cradle, and with theories it was
reared. No wonder that, even when it had
reached manhood, it still retained something of
these early habits of self-conscious, self-critical
production, and appeared somewhat—

Sicklied o'er with the pale cast of thought ;

which does not mean that the German poet, born
in a library, was not to become capable of the fresh-
est and most thrilling utterances as often as he fled
from the dust of his book-shelves into the forests
and the fields of Franconia and Swabia. Yet you
must not forget that this literature was the work
of the learned middle-classes, not of idle and
wealthy gentlemen, but of needy and hard-work-
ing schoolmasters and clergymen. As there was
no great national Court, so there was no rich nobility and gentry to cultivate letters. Nor
was there a *noblesse de robe*, as in France, or
a class of well-to-do merchants, as in England,
who might have filled up their leisure hours
with literary pursuits. Germany boasts of no
Montaigne or Montesquieu, no Shaftesbury or
Bolingbroke. Men of the social position of
Addison and Fielding, of Hume and Gibbon, did
not exist, and, when they existed, did not think of
literature. This, and the seclusion from political

life, and the absence of publicity, gave German literature its particular character, its wonderful freedom from all general fashion, form, style, conventionality, its unique individualism, its daring thought and imagination ; and also its somewhat abstract nature. It sometimes strikes one as a soul without a body. We at once feel that its writers have never known great life, whether social or political. It betrays at the same time a general aversion to action and practical aims, as if the inner life alone had any worth and reality. It was only after the terrible blows which in the beginning of this century awoke them from their dreamy or ideal life, that the Germans began to comprehend that their new intellectual liberty could live and last only in an independent and respected State.

To revert, however, to the literary strifes of the first half of the past century, it was the English tendency which got the better of the contest ; and Richardson was, per- *The English school.* haps, next to Thomson, the writer who contributed most to this result. Clumsy translations of Young's ' Night Thoughts,' followed the heavy metrical versions of ' Paradise Lost,' and the ' Seasons.' Their inspiration was, after all, more

congenial to the German nature, and more adapted
to the social and moral state of the German
middle-class than Racine and Corneille, or even
Molière and Lesage.   Under this influence—for it
is a strange fact that the foundation of a national
culture was still sought through imitation—
and under the tutorship of theoretical criticism,
arose a tame and modest, half-sentimental, half-
moralising sort of literature, which reflected the
petty, prosy, every-day life of the small cities of
Germany, and which pleased because it reflected
it. This humble, timid collection of satires, fables,
and idyls, had, however, the one merit, till now
wanting in all the literary productions of the
country, the merit of depicting German life and
giving expression to German feelings, instead of
describing French and Italian manners, ideas,
and characters.   This literature was certainly as
poor I dare not say poetically, but at least in
rhyme and style as the life it depicted—the
petty customs, defects, weaknesses, and interests
of the poor tutored German middle-class. A host
of Dr. Primroses came forward even before the
English Dr. Primrose came to life; but they were
Primroses without the delightful irony, if not
without the benevolence, of Olivia's father; and

who had never come into contact with gentlemen
like Sir William Thornhill.   Few people read
Gellert's novels, Rabener's satires, Zacharia's
comic poems nowadays; still the historian will find
nowhere a truer image of the modest conditions
of the time than in these pale pictures, which
resemble the bleached old photographs of 1850,
to which we still grant a place in our sitting-
room.

The Seven Years' War soon roused the national
spirit to new life after centuries of slumber.   For
the first time Germans might once more The Seven
feel proud of their deeds, and boast of a Years'War.
national hero ; · and Gleim's ' Grenadiersongs '
(1758) gave vent to this feeling.   The German
' Tyrtœus,' as he was ambitiously called, was a
very mild Tyrtœus, if you like ; still his inspiration
was a more vigorous one than that of the timid
and sentimental friends of his youth.   Together
with him, however, appeared on the field the
somewhat younger generation of the great intellectual warriors who definitively freed the
German mind from the foreign yoke and the
bondage of narrow tradition, and who cleared
the ground upon which those who followed were
to build.

Our new literature only began properly towards 1760. The hundred preceding years were Recapitulation. entirely filled with the slow and wearisome process of recovery from the material misery and the intellectual, as well as moral decay in which the Thirty Years' War had left us. It required these hundred years before people could attain even that modest degree of well-being which allowed them to give a thought to something else than the care for material existence. It required these hundred years to free German Religion, as well as German Science, from the thraldom of orthodox theology. It required these hundred years to create the beginnings only of a national State, and to reform some, at least, of the abuses of the Empire. It required yet a hundred years more of incessant toil, and four generations of men of genius and of talent, to bring about a really national literature and a really national State, looked up to and respected by the world. No doubt, as this our new State still bears the stamp of its origin—the bureaucratical and military monarchy of Frederick the Great,— so our new literature, very different in this respect from our literature of the Middle Ages, as well as from that of the sixteenth century, is a literature of scholars and officials. It reflects the intellectual and moral life of that class. It does not depict a large social and public life, which did not exist when it sprang up, and which has scarcely come even now, when all has been done that was necessary to clear the ground for it—perhaps because our history, our intellectual and moral aptitudes, make us less fit than other nations for such a life, and assign to us other and by no means lower fields of activity. Be this as it may, you will never understand our political and literary conditions if you forget the starting-point of modern Germany; if you do not remember that, whereas the German of the sixteenth century was fully on a par with the Englishman, Frenchman, and Italian, in material and intellectual, as well as in moral and social, respects, the German of the seventeenth century was thrown back into utter barbarism by the Thirty Years' War. When our country, at the end of that cruel time, towards 1650, set out on a new career, she had everything to rebuild anew; state and religion, wealth and society, science and literature, language, even, and morality. The start of two hundred years, which western Europe thus had over Germany, is still apparent in our society and manners, in our

wealth and comfort. We have the presumption
to believe that intellectually and morally—politically, also, since 1866, if we do not cling to the
prejudice that parliamentary government is the
only one worthy of a civilised nation—we have
again come up with our western neighbours in
the great race of civilisation, in which men are
not rivals but fellow-workers.

LECTURE III.

THE SEEDS OF GERMAN THOUGHT.

(1760–1770.)

It was during, and shortly after, the Seven Years' War (1756 to 1763) that the first generation of the great founders of our national culture made their appearance.

There are three generations, indeed, which followed each other at twenty years' distance, and which almost entirely did the great work of German culture, of which I have undertaken to trace the outlines in these short lectures. The first, born between 1715 and 1735, the generation of Klopstock, Wieland, Winckelmann, Kant, Mendelssohn, above all, Lessing, whose principal works were published between 1750 and 1770, when these men were from thirty to fifty years old. The second generation, born in the middle of the century, included Herder and Voss, Klinger and Bürger, Goethe and Schiller,

The three generations.

whose greatest and most fertile activity displayed itself equally during their full manhood, from 1770 to 1800. Finally, in the third generation, born be-- tween 1760 and 1780, the most conspicuous names were those of the two Schlegels, the two Humboldts, Tieck, Rahel, Schleiermacher, Niebuhr, Savigny and Schelling, whose followers acted more parti- cularly in the first quarter of the present century. The two schools which, from 1825, to 1850, influenced the German mind most powerfully, the school of Hegel and that of Gervinus, only con- tinued, developed, summed up, applied, or contra- dicted the main ideas of the three preceding great generations ; they did not properly put forth and circulate new ideas.

It was a manly and robust generation, the generation of Klopstock, Wieland, Lessing, which was also that of Frederick, Winckelmann, and Kant. They almost all were born in the humblest stations of life, and fought their way through direst privation ; but the struggle for life was not capable of stifling in them the sense of the ideal.

You all know how Klopstock was formed by
Klopstock, born 1724.
English, Wieland by French models. They were, however, no servile imitators ; and .they are thus distinguished from the Brockes

and Gottscheds of the preceding age. They
filled their works with a spirit of their own, and
modified even the forms which they borrowed, so
as to accommodate them to the genius of their
own language. The tendency of their age was
still that of the beginning of the century: a
deeply religious spirit, but one which believed more
in the continuous revelation of God through conscience than in the historical revelation of the
Orthodox, or the argumentation of the Deists,
representing God as the great architect of this
material machine. It was partly because Klopstock
gave a poetical expression to this feeling that his
poem acted so powerfully; and partly also because
its form seemed an entirely German one, although
the verse was the classical hexameter of the
ancients, now for the first time quite assimilated
and mastered, as that generation believed. Germany imagined that she too possessed a 'Paradise
Lost,' and welcomed in the bard of the 'Messiah'
the interpreter of its innermost thought. Then at
last Germany had a German poem, both in substance and form; and neither substance nor form
was of the mediocre, prosy, and humble kind to
which German genius seemed till then condemned.
Thought and language soared high too high,

G

perhaps, for us to follow it still with our clipped
wings—yet it proved to the nation that she might
attempt what other nations had successfully attempted before her.

Whilst Klopstock's inspiration was Christian
and Teutonic, that of Wieland was more ration-
Wieland, alistic and cosmopolitan. If Klopstock
born 1733. taught the German language strength
and flight, Wieland gave it fluency and elegance.
He became, indeed, the very creator of a simple,
easy, and natural prose, the most necessary instrument of culture. German prose before Wieland
was pedantic, stiff, intricate : with some writers
it is so still. Wieland gave it the tone of polite
society ; taught it how to handle irony, how
to be witty with grace and decorum. He himself had belonged entirely to the school of the
French, particularly to that of Voltaire, and
among the English, Shaftesbury, the *virtuoso*, had
been the chief object of his study and predilection.
When he wrote his philosophical novels and minor
poems in Voltaire's manner, Germany seemed at
first astonished to see that her heavy language
could be capable of such charming, prattling talk.
Wieland won over to it the higher classes, then
exclusively bred in French ; he made German lan-

guage and literature *hoffähig* (admissible at Court).
At the same time he popularised the English and
French philosophy of the time. The popular
philosophers of Berlin, such as Mendelssohn and
Nicolaï, the friends of Lessing, would have been
impossible without Wieland; and their influence
was great. As Klopstock and his followers had
given a poetical expression to the religious feeling
of the nation, independent of, and superior to,
dogma and outward worship, so Wieland directed
the war of the century against sacerdotalism and
theology with the somewhat blunted, but not less
effective, arms, which German free-thought has
ever since used against Church and dogma; for
Germany seemed to have found at least the proper
vehicle to enable her to join in the movement of
Western culture, instead of following it at a distance. Now, only, she seemed to have made that
culture completely her own.

This was necessary; but it was not sufficient. She wanted also to be able to go on alone
and without anybody's help. She was no longer
the province of a foreign civilisation, but she was
still a tributary. And she had to be freed from this
allegiance also, and to be received on an equal footing in the intellectual society of Europe, before she

could work on her own account.   More than this :
after having obtained an entire command over
foreign culture, after having not only accepted
but digested and assimilated it, it became necessary that she should react against it : for all life-
bringing movement is action and reaction.

Lessing undertook the task.   It was he who
founded the literary independence of Germany

Lessing,
born 1729.

by rebelling against the foreign laws,
which had remained even after the foreign
rulers had yielded the place to home-born leaders ;
and he freed, not Germany alone, but the whole
world, when he gave the deadly blow to the conventional classicism of the French.   For it is hard to
believe that Byron, Manzoni, Victor Hugo himself
could have written what they wrote, without
Lessing's 'Dramaturgie ' ?   When Lessing attacked
the French poetical laws and rules, they were still
universally acknowledged.   Addison had written
his 'Cato ' in conformity with them, and Pope
recognisèd no higher authority ; and, long after
them, Moratin preferred Racine to his own Calderon, as *they* had placed Corneille over Shakespeare.   Nay, even after Lessing, but before his
influence could be felt on the other side of the
Alps, Alfieri, the *Misogallo*, cast his impetuous

thought in the French mould. Lessing was the
first revolt against that law, and to show that it was
entirely conventional and arbitrary, adhering to
outward and accidental forms, instead of to the
essence of ancient poetry. From Boileau's theories
he appealed to Aristotle, from Corneille's practice
to that of Shakespeare, whom he proved to be a
truer, although unconscious, follower of Sophocles
than Corneille. But Aristotle himself and Shakespeare he treated as a true Protestant treats the
Bible : with the spirit of free inquiry. He did
not submit to Aristotle because he was Aristotle,
but because he discovered in him ' truth as sure
as that of Euclid.'

At the same time, adding example to theory,
he gave to Germany literary works of his own at
once popular and refined, such as she had yearned
for so long. He united Wieland's realism with
Klopstock's idealism in works which have survived,
whilst those of Klopstock and Wieland can scarcely
be said to be still living. He gave a model of the
free dramatic form, which he wanted to substitute
for the French pattern, in his ' Emilia Galotti.'
He gave words to the first national enthusiasm
felt by modern Germany at Frederick's deeds in
his ' Minna von Barnhelm.' Nay, the whole re-

ligious and philosophical creed of his generation
he expressed in his 'Nathan,' for which his friend
Mendelssohn sat as model, and which he left as
a legacy to the nation, to the world. The spirit ·
of toleration, together with a firm belief in a good
and just Deity, breathes in every page of that
wonderful work, in which the best ideas of the age
are summed up. For what he had done for literature he did for religion; what he had done for
Aristotle he did for Luther. 'The true Lutheran,' he exclaimed, ' does not want to be
protected by Luther's writings, but by Luther's
spirit, and Luther's spirit exacts absolutely that
no man should be prevented from communicating
his progress in knowledge to others.' He would
not allow the Protestant clergy to assume an
authority which the spirit of Protestantism for-
bids them to claim, and declared loudly that he
would be ' the first to take back the Pope for the
popelings' if they should put a stop to free
inquiry. And as his ' Nathan ' showed religious
feeling to be independent of, and superior to,
established forms of religion, so in his ' Education
of Mankind ' he showed that morality is independent even of religious belief; and that the good done
for the satisfaction of one's own conscience is

superior to that which is done with a hope of re-
compense in a future life, the preoccupation of
such a life being rather an impediment than a
furtherance towards making the best use of this
existence. 'Why not quietly wait for a future
life, as one waits for the morrow?' without wish-
ing to investigate what cannot be investigated,
the things which it will bring? Who knows
whether there will not come 'a new eternal gospel,'
promised in the New Testament, and which will
be to Christianity what Christianity was to Juda-
ism, a third stage in the long education of mankind by God, for whom 'the shortest line is not
always a straight line'? In such ideas, however,
Lessing was far in advance of his generation, for
he not only gave the last expression to the past,
but he also opened the door for the coming age.
He, as well as Kant and Winckelmann, stood
with his feet in the eighteenth century; with
his head he already reached the nineteenth.

Winckelmann had published his 'History of
Art' in 1764; so had Kant his 'Observations on
the Sublime.' In 1766, just a hundred years
before the auspicious birthday of the German
State, appeared his 'Dreams of a Visionary,'
Winckelmann's 'Allegory,' Lessing's 'Laocoon.'

and the most suggestive book perhaps ever written, Herder's 'Fragments.' They announced to the world that the years' of apprenticeship were over for Germany, and that she had begun to work on her own account.

The medium through which the modern classical writers of the Italian and French type looked at antiquity was Roman civilisation. Ever since the Jesuits had become masters of public education in the neo-Latin countries, they had seen how easy it would be in nations, whose Church, whose language, and whose legal traditions were Roman, to put the Latin literature in the foreground. They felt at the same time how important for their aim it would be to mould men's minds by Roman antiquity, the spirit of which is discipline, instead of feeding them with Greek antiquity, the essence of which is freedom. While the contemporaries of Angelo Poliziano and Marsilio Ficino still lived under the charm of the Hellenic civilisation, those of Bembo and Alamanni were already under the spell of Latin Alexandrinism.

Lessing had been as attentive a reader of Sophocles as of Shakespeare; and when he proposed the latter instead of Corneille as a model to the future dramatic poets of Germany, it was

View of antiquity.

because he saw in him, in spite of his irregular form, a more faithful, if not a more systematic follower of the ancients, than in Racine and Corneille. Here also it was not the letter which he preached, but the spirit. He protested against the whole way of looking at the ancients, which had reigned ever since Trissino and Tasso, as against a sort of third Alexandrinism. For, according to him, they saw the importance of ancient literature where it was not, in accidental outward forms; and sacrificed to these that which had really inspired the ancients—natural beauty. He wished his age and his nation to do what the great artists of the Renaissance had done, before academical classicism had set in, viz., to look on Nature and Man directly with clear, sound, unprejudiced eyes, such as the Greeks had brought to the contemplation of things; and to create, if necessary, new forms for new thoughts and feelings. It is highly important to notice that a new view of antiquity, entirely opposed to the academical one, was the basis of the literary edifice which Germany was about to build. Hence also the importance of Winckelmann's 'History of Art,' which, as I have said, appeared in 1764, and of his 'Allegory' which was published in 1766.

Winckelmann's 'History of Art' is at once a
system of æsthetics and a history. There may be,

Winckel-
mann, born
1717. and there are, many points on which we
are at variance with Winckelmann, and
the fundamental idea even of his great
book—that the aim of art is the creation of ideal
forms—is no longer, I hope, admitted by æsthetic
criticism. Nevertheless, his book acted as if it
was a revelation of the Hellenic world. Winckelmann had himself something of the spirit of the
Greeks, and so became naturally their most eloquent interpreter. It was as if he had brushed
away the dust from the ancients, and revealed
to view the purity of their outlines, buried as they
were under a dense layer of rubbish. He endeavoured to show in language hitherto unparal-
leled—a prose lofty and noble, nay, majestic, without affectation, and correct without purism—in a
language worthy of the ancients, that the Greek
art of the time of Pericles rested on the same basis
as the Platonic philosophy ; the basis of idealism,
contemplating the real world as a reflection of the
world of ideas, and trying to reconstruct for the
senses, as Plato tried to do for the intellect, those
ideas which were like the lost types of the created
world. Against the unquiet, overladen style of
his own time, he invoked the calm and simplicity

of Greek art, even introducing into painting the
rules of sculpture. Although this reaction against
rococo degenerated soon—as all reactions will do—
and degenerated into the cold and dry school of a
new Academy, almost worse than the Berninesque
school which it superseded, yet it was a necessary
reaction, and one which, if it has done no good in
the domain of the fine arts, has had most fertile results for poetry. Goethe's ' Iphigenia,' and ' Alexis
and Dora,' would never have been written, if
Winckelmann had not first unveiled the ideal
beauty of Greek antiquity. The powdered and
patched Greek heroines of Voltaire's tragedy became henceforward as impossible as the sentimental or raging heroes of Crébillon. For they
were totally devoid of that ' noble simplicity and
calm grandeur ' which Winckelmann had established as the first principle of Greek art. If men
like David and Ingres, Canova and Thorwaldsen,
who were directly or indirectly disciples of
Winckelmann, proved themselves unable to create
an Iphigenia, at once Greek and modern, ideal
and real, full of life and full of measure, it was
because the generation to which they belonged
entirely lacked the natural disposition which
makes great artists, that spontaneous, direct
intuition, which is unbiassed by abstract thought

and abstract systems. It was also—I will not
deny it—because the new theory could not be accepted throughout. Sculpture had tried to produce
the effects of painting. Winckelmann went into
the other extreme by introducing into painting
the rules of sculpture. But, we have not to
ask ourselves here whether the action of Winckelmann was beneficial or not; only what it was, and
how far it reached.

But Winckelmann did even more in his History
than reveal the principle of Greek Art. He
gave the first example of modern historical
method. All histories of Art, like those of
literature, had been till then collections of biogra-
phies, lists of titles, and analyses or descriptions
of different works, with an account of their vicissitudes. Winckelmann was not only the first to dis-
tinguish the different periods of Art as coinciding
with the different styles; he also described its
growth and decay as if it were a natural vegetation,
showed the causes of this growth and decay--
climate, national character and national manners,
political history, religion, race—and thus restored
the unity of History. Thus Winckelmann first
introduced, not in theory, but in practice, the idea
of organic and historical development, which is pro-

perly *the* German idea. In his hands the history
of the infancy, adolescence, youth, maturity, and
old age of Art became a system of the different
styles, and *vice versâ*. He expelled the conception of arbitrary creation by intellects independent
of circumstances from the domain of Art-history ;
and it was only after Winckelmann had shown Fine
Arts to be the result of the general condition of a
given civilisation, that other writers began to apply
the same idea to Poetry, Philosophy, Religion and
the State. The first seed of the German idea was
thrown into the world.

But although Winckelmann had awakened the
sense for the ' noble simplicity and calm grandeur '
of ancient Art, he had not been able to
divest himself of certain intellectual
habits of his time. As he had proposed ideal
forms as the highest aim of Art, *i.e.* forms which
do not exist in nature, but are the product of the
idealising mind, and had combined the fruits of his
various observations into one patchwork called
ideal beauty, so he had raised no objection against
abstract thought becoming the object of Art, in
other words, against allegory. This was the
legacy of the French rationalistic culture of the
first half of the century against which Lessing

Lessing's
' Laocoon.'

was to lead the reaction. The French of that time approached Poetry as they approached Religion, as they approached the State, with the conviction that the organ of understanding was able to produce intentionally and consciously what in reality has always been the product of other human faculties acting almost unconsciously; they believed in inventors of religion as in inventors of constitutions. Hence a confusion of all the activities of the human mind. People believed that the Fine Arts could serve to explain abstract thought, which is allegory, and again that words might paint objects, which produced descriptive poetry. The simple explanation that words, sounds, forms, and colours are different languages for different orders of mental activity had been entirely lost sight of. Experience taught that none of these mental faculties could work when isolated, without the aid of the others; the inference was drawn that each might do the work of the other. People wanted to express in forms and colours, that is, in the language of the Fine Arts, what can only be expressed in words; and they wanted to express in words what can only be expressed in sounds, *i.e.* music. The great historical importance of Lessing's ' Laocoon ' lies in the fact that it put a stop

once for all to that confusion—once for all, if everybody had known how to read it, or had consented
to read it as it was written. We should not have
musicians who are content to interpret words, or
painters who condescend to illustrate novels and
poems, if the necessary consequences had been
drawn from Lessing's premises. For in his comparison between Virgil's description of Laocoon's
death and the famous group in the Vatican,
he traced the impassable boundary which separates Fine Arts and Poetry. The Fine Arts
have to show things in space and to the eyes,
Poetry in time and through the ears to the intellect: the inference is that the subjects of the
Fine Arts must be circumscribed objects, or,
at least, lasting situations as extended in space
and capable of being embraced in one glance,
whereas the subjects of poetry must be actions
accomplished in time, and conveyed to the
intellect in their successive stages. When, consequently, the poet wants to treat the same subject
as the artist, he must first transform it into action,
as Homer did with Achilles' shield and Helen's
beauty (her appearance before and impression on
the old men of Troy); or Goethe, when he describes
the gardens of Hermann's father, by following

the steps of his mother from one part to the
other. If, on the contrary, the artist wishes to
treat a poetical subject, he must first transform
the action into a situation of some duration. As a
rule it would be better still to avoid such a subject
altogether ; but if he does take it he must first
modify it, choosing in the action that moment
which is most lasting and at the same time most
pregnant, *i.e.* in which there is contained most of
the past and of the coming moment.

There is much to object to in this theory which
would condemn altogether such masterpieces as
Rubens' *Lionhunt* or Géricault's *Hussars*, and is
not only, as it seems to me, a most insufficient definition of the artistic object, but also leaves un-
touched the far more important side of the question,
viz., the subjective origin of a work of art. On
the whole we should be justified in saying that
Lessing's artistic education was very incomplete,
his artistic organisation, if he had any, hardly at
all developed. This, in fact, is somewhat the fault
of all the German æsthetic theories which have been
brought forward during the last hundred years;
nay, Lessing, who saw the point in poetry so ad-
mirably, still harboured the false and hollow conception of the ideal which was the principal mis-

take of Winckelmann. Be this, however, as it
may, I am not here to criticise, but to explain,
and I turn again to Lessing's proper field, literature, where his thought was to bear fruit a hundredfold. The essence of poetry, Lessing taught,
is action; but action which reveals the complete-
ness of human nature, and which must therefore
show man in the free movement of passion.
The aim of poetry, then, is to reproduce human
passions, and to inspire sympathy with them,
but a sympathy purely human, free from all
personal interest; and, as poetry is not to
produce in us real, material fear and hope,
so it does not pursue either moral or religious or
political aims: it has its aim in itself. 'True
Art' (*Darstellung*), says Goethe, 'has no aim; it
neither approves nor disapproves; it develops the
feelings and actions as they follow each other and
out of each other, and by this, and this alone, it
enlightens and teaches.' With this the didactic
poem was banished from literature, as the descriptive had been banished from it by the former
theory. And this was the second seed sown between 1760 and 1770.

If Winckelmann and Lessing reacted against
the æsthetic views of the French, Kant and

H

Herder received their first impulse from them :
Kant, born 1724. not from Voltaire, it is true, nor from the Encyclopædists (with the exception of Diderot, who differed from them in many respects, and had immense influence on German thought), but principally from Buffon and Rousseau. In his metaphysical thought Kant rests entirely on Newton.' He started from Locke and Hume in his psychology, which overthrew all metaphysics as they had been taught till then. In his views of history and humanity, with which we are more especially concerned here, he owed as much to Rousseau, although he reacted partly against him, as he did against Hume's psychology. This he only developed twenty years later, thereby producing in philosophical science a revolution only to be compared with that effected by Newton in the natural sciences; but they belong to the periods which we shall have to consider in our fifth lecture. To-day we must fix our attention on the Kant of 1766, not the Kant of 1787. Till then, as he shows in his 'Natural History of the Heavens,' which was inspired by Newton, Kant considered the history of mankind, somewhat like that of nature, in the light of a deadly struggle for life. Just as our planet through terrible cata-

strophes and cataclysms had shaped itself into a
dwelling for reasonable beings, so humanity advances through wars and revolutions towards perfection; and just as nature emerges more and
more out of chaos into organisation, so the human
mind frees itself more and more from the tumult
of blind passions, and through perfecting of the
intellect forms a pure image of the eternal harmony of the universe. Few individuals, however,
attain this lofty aim; the great majority vegetate like plants; millions of germs perish; the
progress of humanity takes place only in the high
spheres of a privileged few.

This aristocratic belief was deeply shaken by
the reading of Rousseau's works towards 1760.
Rousseau, as you all remember, saw in the progress
of art and science the cause of immorality as well
as of inequality among men. He represented the
natural state of man as good, and contended that
his superiority over animals was not in his intelligence, but in his heart. Now, as feeling is not,
like intelligence, the privilege of a few, as it is
the common possession of men, the whole democratic view of Rousseau results from this deceptive
paradox. Kant adopted this theory, though in a
modified form, in his 'Considerations on the Senti-

ment of the Beautiful and the Sublime,' which
appeared in 1764, eight years after Burke's
work on the same subject, with which, however, it
has much less in common than with Lessing's
'Laocoon.' According to Kant's correction of
Rousseau's views, it is no longer the intellectual
culture of privileged classes or individuals which
is the aim of history, but the culture of the
masses through the education of their feelings.
In this respect he allows that a retrograde movement has taken place, which is also a progressive one—retrograde compared with Greek antiquity ; progressive compared with the savage state
of primitive tribes. For he holds that the perfection of human nature was realised in the simple
civilisation of the ancients, and by no means
shares Rousseau's enthusiasm for savages.
He preaches a return to nature, but finds nature,
not in the primitive times which knew no
art and no thought, but, like Winckelmann,
in the Hellenic civilisation which had remained
faithful to nature. There, indeed, was a union of
true nature and true culture, and Kant hoped that
humanity might come again to such a state through
a simpler education ; nay, he believed that it *will*
be the final result of all the warfare and movement

of history. No doubt, man only acts within the given limits of nationality, epoch, and climate; but he must strive, and will strive with success, to develop more and more the purely human in himself. National distinctions will not, therefore, disappear; only they will be no longer contrasts, but merely varieties and gradations of character— a view which was entirely accepted by Lessing and Herder, Goethe and Schiller, and has remained *the* German view of cosmopolitanism and nationality. Kant goes a step farther on the way to which Rousseau had directed him.

The motive power in Nature is pleasure and pain, the sensation of what furthers and what impedes the development of life. But in man a whole series of more delicate sensations is added to those of pleasure and pain : the sensations of ideal worth, sensations which are less strong but more durable than the material ones. Such is the feeling of honour—an inferior feeling still, because it depends upon the judgment of others and implies a selfish personal interest. Such is sympathy, which is above all selfish personal interest—nay, is the contradiction of it—but lacks duration and consistency. Such is above all the feeling of duty, which makes us sacrifice our personal interest, not

according to momentary impulse, but to a fixed
and durable rule of conduct. It has its origin in
the feeling of one's own dignity, which dignity we
grant to every other human being, and which we
respect in him; for man, who lives in conformity
with nature, both esteems himself and considers
every human being as a fellow-creature deserving
esteem. This feeling once awakened, the beauty
of the soul becomes the highest æsthetic and
moral ideal. Among the moderns, the Italians
through fine art, the French through elegance and
taste, the English through earnestness and depth,
have come nearest to this ideal. 'By their feeling
of duty, by their unbending fidelity to principles,
by their enthusiasm for the rights and dignity of
man, the English set an example to all nations.'
The Germans follow slowly in the cultivation of
æsthetic and moral feeling. Once freed and cured
of their present vices, leading a free and national
life, they will perhaps unite the virtues of the
French and English, delicacy of taste and a strong
sense of duty; and a new Hellenic life will blossom
once more. This hope, this ideal, animated
the whole of this and the next generation. Germany was to become a new Greece; humanism
in the highest sense, intellectual, moral, and

social, was to be realised by her. But none at that
time, except Kant and Herder, saw clearly what
was the preliminary condition for such a second
Renaissance. 'What is wanting to our country,'
said Herder, almost at the same moment as Kant,
' is public feeling, a noble pride, which is not to be
organised according to foreign patterns, but will
organise itself according to its own nature, as
other nations have always done: to be Germans
on our own well-defended soil.'

So spoke the fourth of the German prophets,
Herder. He was the first to draw out the consequences involved in the teaching of his master,
Kant, that the purely human was the aim of history
and culture, a teaching which we ought to consider
as the seed which, next to Winckelmann's and
Lessing's, worked most powerfully on the German
mind. True, Kant's earlier writings (although
composed in a style of such eloquence that the
reader sometimes wonders how the same hand
could have written in the dry and abstract style of
the ' Critic of Judgment ') did not waken so loud an
echo as the contemporary works of Winckelmann,
Lessing, and Herder. Still they fell on good
ground, and proved in the long run as fertile as,
perhaps more fertile than, the seeds sown by his
contemporaries.

I have pronounced the name of Herder, and I have called him a prophet. Such a name he indeed deserves more, perhaps, than any man of the last century. He had the soul and he had the language of a seer, and it was as a seer that he worked upon his contemporaries. In reality he belongs to the next generation, although his first work appeared at the same moment as the writings, which I have noticed, of Winckelmann, Lessing, and Kant. He was only twenty-two, and an obscure teacher in the distant Baltic provinces under Russian rule, when his 'Fragmente' appeared in 1766, and ran through Germany with the quickness of a train of gunpowder. With him, then, the new generation made its entrance. Older than Goethe, Bürger, Jacobi, Voss, by four or five years only, he became their master at once, the preacher of the new literary gospel, to whom they listened as if he had been inspired.

It is perhaps—nay, it is certainly— a great disadvantage that I should have chosen a subject and adopted a plan of treating it, which obliges me to pass by the men and their lives, their moral character, their living persons, and to present to you only their ideas, detached from life like fruits from the tree : their ideas, moreover, in an

Herder, born 1744.

abstract form and condensed in a few words. Still
the subject is so vast, and our time so short, that
I must needs thus confine myself, however dry
and unattractive my subject must consequently
become. I regret it often, however, and never
can I regret it more than when I speak of Herder,
who was neither a great writer, nor a great in-
vestigator and discoverer, nor an accomplished
poet, but who was a mighty personality and whose
doctrine itself was, so to speak, the doctrine of
personality.

No one, Kant perhaps alone excepted, has contributed more to the stock of German thought,
or has ever exercised greater or more lasting
influence over an age, a nation, or the world
at large than Herder. Like the genuine rebel
he was, he began by turning upside down the
science and literature which then reigned, as
Kant was to do with the philosophical speculation
of his time.   He was a revolutionist indeed.
Lessing would fain have paused after having freed
the laws of composition from the hoary over-
growth of time, false interpretation, and erroneous
application. He never had the slightest intention
of attacking the laws themselves. But, however
great a man's genius may be, he cannot stem at

his will the current which carries away a whole
generation with it—particularly when he has
himself cleared the road for it by removing the
obstacles which stood in its way.   Every Mirabeau
finds a Danton to outstep him.   Lessing had
claimed the right of individual genius to modify
rule, and five years had hardly elapsed after the
publication of his 'Dramaturgie' when the
literary *montagne* already urged a radical abolition of all literary legislation and proclaimed the
right of genius to absolute self-government.
Reform had drifted into revolution; and Herder
was marching at the head of the insurgents.

Before showing the influence exercised by
Herder over his contemporaries, let us see what
was the nature of the new principle applied by
him to theology, history, and poetry.   It was the
superiority of nature over civilisation, and of intuition over reason.   The essence of Herder's
ideas lay in continually opposing synthesis to
analysis, the individual to rule, spontaneous impulse to conscious action, organism to mechan-
ism, development and growth to legislation and
creation—in a word, in placing the *fieri* above
the *facere*.   This was the basis of the creed
professed by that school of 'original geniuses'

which he was leading to battle against the
religious, literary, and scientific rationalism of the
age.

No man finds his starting-point within himself.
The starting-point of German thought was in
France, as that of French thought had been in
England. It was more particularly from Rousseau
that Herder received his first impulse. Rousseau's
The reaction against the exclusive wor- Influence.
ship of reason had begun precisely in those
countries,which had been foremost in establishing
it. It was the land of Pope and Hume which
gave birth to Burns and Burke; and the writings
of Lowth and Wood, of Young and Macpherson
had struck out in literature and criticism that
path on which Rousseau was to lead the latter
half of the century in political and social matters.
Mankind was to return to nature, to that good
parent whose works had become disfigured by the
manners and customs of a polished, refined society.
It is difficult for us in our days to form any adequate conception of the effect produced by Rousseau's 'Discourse on Inequality' at the time when
it appeared. 'It is impossible to speak otherwise
than with secret veneration of these lofty ideas
and sublime thoughts,' exclaimed Lessing, then

a young man, but already very little disposed to
be sentimental. Kant actually forgot his daily
walk while he perused ' Emile.' Even ten years
later, Schiller compared Rousseau to Socrates—
' Rousseau, who perished by the hands of Christians; Rousseau, who would fain make human
beings out of Christians.' Herder, while yet a
student, addressed enthusiastic verses to Rousseau,
in which he chose him for ' his guide through life.'
One must read the description which Goethe has
left of the impression made on the youth of Germany by Rousseau's works. What it was in
France is well known. We smile at those diminutive
English parks which replaced Le Notre's stately
avenues, at the farmyards established in royal de-
mesnes, and at the queens who turned themselves
into dairymaids. When we read of the great
ladies of the eighteenth century suckling their
infants amidst a group of *élégants*, we are often
tempted to see more affectation in it than there
really was. Everything in that powdered and
hooped company had become so artificial that any
symptom of naturalism appeared as a deliverance,
passed for a protest against unnatural refinement,
and really was a thoroughly justified reaction
against the opposite extreme. Nothing, indeed,

could be more justifiable than Rousseau's opposition to Voltaire and the Encyclopædists; for
what was it but the rebellion of feeling against
reason which till then had restrained and en-
thralled it—of feeling which burst the tight
ligatures by which men had sought to confine
their hearts, in the effort to shake off reason's
yoke and obtain breathing room for itself?

In Germany too, the spirit of the 'Encyclo-
pædia' was then reigning, or at least threaten-
ing to reign. The great Frederick, Nicolai and his
followers in Berlin, Wieland himself, were confirmed rationalists at heart, although the rationalism of the latter was draped in Shaftesbury's
æsthetical epicurism. We find common sense,
not sentiment, ruling all things. Even in
Mendelssohn and Lessing, although their inspiration is so different from that of the
French and English rationalists, light is · the
characteristic quality. How should such minds,
in which everything was clearness, precision,
and accuracy, have any room left for vague twilight? Now, that same precise, matter of fact,
uncompromising thing which we denominate
common sense never did engender poetry, and
chiaroscuri will exist in the depths of man's

nature. Such things as dim apprehensions, pre-
sentiments, *réverie,* lie dormant within the innermost recesses of the human soul—nay, form,
mayhap, the most precious of its treasures. If
we seek to light up these dark corners, not by
the mild and unfailing light of inward revelation
or intuition, but by the dazzling and often mis-
leading lantern of reason, we may chase from their
haunts the spirits which have taken up their abode
there. Then, as often happens, we may only succeed in driving them to seek refuge in mystery
elsewhere, and to assume the form of a grosser
superstition, while, if wholly cast out, they leave
behind them a blank void together with a
painful longing to fill it up again. An Aene-
sidemus provokes an Apollonius of Tyana;
and the d'Holbachs and Helvetiuses are followed
by the Cagliostros and Mesmers. Herein lay
Herder's right of protest against the prose of
common sense, as against the moralising didacti-
cism of German poetry, from which even Lessing
was unable entirely to free his contemporaries,
and against the petrified forms of citizen life,
religion and science in Germany; for Herder's
protest against one-sided rationalism never degenerated into a defence of superstition or mysticism.

Whereas Rousseau had chiefly sought to re-establish nature's rights in social matters, Herder wished to establish them in things of the intellect. In that lies his originality. It was by this he developed and continued what Rousseau had begun, and it was by this that he was finally induced to turn round upon Rousseau and react against him. While searching for nature's unconscious proceeding in her intellectual creation of what we call language, religion, and poetry, he ended by discovering the secret of her process in creating society and the state, and found this process to be the antipodes of the *Contrat Social.* You will find in Herder's earliest writings the ideas developed twenty-five years later in Burke's 'Reflections.' [1]

But it was not Rousseau alone who acted upon Herder and his master Hamann, 'the Magician of the North,' as they used to call him. Herder's mind was stirred by the English works on Homer, by the poetry of the Bible, by Shakespeare, by Percy's ballads; as he was also im-

Herder's Principles.

---

[1] Mr. Leslie Stephen and Mr. John Morley have abundantly proved that Burke expressed this fundamental belief of his life as early as 1756 in his *Vindication of Natural Society* ; but he expressed it *en passant* without developing it, and without finding an echo, as he did thirty-five years later, and as Herder did from the outset.

pressed by Buffon's profound views of nature
and the cohesion of intellectual and physical life.
Still it was Rousseau's idea, that the condition
of human development lay in the enlightenment
and perfecting, not of our reasoning faculty, but
of our feelings, which led him to investigate
the elementary operations of the soul. These
operations soon assumed in his eyes the character
of infallible powers. Instinctive, intuitive man,
with all the energies of body and mind unimpaired,
became the ideal man.   Everybody and everything was to be looked at, not dissolved, as
abstract philosophy had dissolved it, into its parts
by analysis, nor detached from the natural circumstances, but in the combination of the parts
in an indivisible whole.   So everybody was to
act.   Coherence, cohesion became the watch-
word. Not isolated faculties, but only all the
faculties combined, could grasp the outward as
well as the inner world. Intuition is all. Æsthetic rules as well as moral laws ought to be put
aside.   Even in science sight is to replace analysis.
Here we have the germ of that contrast between
Herder and Kant which was to break out so much
later.   Indeed, both Kant and Herder gave
definitive and systematic shape to their ideas only

twenty years later, and, although starting from the same point, reached very different conclusions. So did Goethe and Schiller, whose poetical production began under the powerful influence of Herder's views, but was afterwards deeply modified through Kant and a more methodical study of nature. To-day we only contemplate their spring, which was the spring also of German intellectual life—a spring full, of course, like all springs, of promises which were not kept; full of terrible storms also, which, however, proved to be salutary in the end; full, above all, of a charming freshness which the literature of summer did not find again.

Herder himself, the mighty representative of this age—he in whose work all the new ideas which have animated the intellectual world during fifty years are in germ—Herder himself remained always a youth, ever unable to give a definite and artistically measured form to his thought. Herder's very universality was injurious to him. His range was too vast to allow of his grasping anything firmly : *il embrassa trop pour bien étreindre.* His ever-wandering eye never could restrict itself to one narrow spot, and his enthusiasm reminds us more of a burning steppe than the concen-

I

trated, persistent glow of a furnace. He caught
glimpses — I might almost say he had the visions
of a genius, upon all subjects, mastering none
completely; and thus, while able to give the
architect the most valuable suggestions, he was
himself utterly at a loss to construct the smallest
edifice. No man ever scattered abroad a greater
quantity of fruitful seeds than he; yet at the
close of his career he found that he had not
tilled a single corner of his own field according to
rule. It is undeniable that his works are more
remarkable for the variety than for the profundity
of the learning they contain, as he himself was
endowed with more imagination than good sense,
with more ardour than thoroughness.

It was precisely these defects, nevertheless,
which determined his immense and immediate

Herder's
action. influence. He was certainly one of the
greatest incentive powers the world has
ever known. 'Who is this modern Pindar who
has just made his appearance amongst you?'
wrote Winckelmann from Rome in 1767, when
Herder's ' Fragments ' had just appeared. ' This,
to be sure, is a madman or a genius,' exclaimed
Wieland. ' Whoever may be the author,' Lessing
said to Nicolaï, ' he is at any rate the only one for

whom it is worth *my* while to publish my ideas.'
If the mature generation spoke thus, what must
have been the effect of the youthful prophet upon
the unripe one? Nor is the fact astonishing. By
dint of analysing human nature, and introducing
into history the division of labour, people had
come to such a point that, as Mephistopheles has
it, 'they held the parts in their hands, the intellectual link alone being wanting.' It was Herder's
unmethodical visionary imagination which discovered the failing link, and reunited what analysis
had severed.

'Everything that man undertakes to produce,
whether by action, word, or in whatsoever way,
ought to spring from the union of all his faculties.
All that is isolated is condemnable.' These are the
words in which Goethe sums up the fundamental
idea which inspired Herder's master Hamann and
Herder himself. Nothing, he would say, is in
reality isolated, and just as each individual sense
is assisted by the four others in the perception of
any object which absorbs our attention, so do
memory and imagination likewise co-operate with
judgment and perception in enabling us to acquire
our knowledge of things. This union of all the
faculties, this primitive entireness of the individual,

is what we must endeavour to recover, such as it was in the early ages, ere abstract rules had been thought of—times when each individual acted, thought, and spoke according to inspiration and direct view. And what is true of individuals is true of nations. What they produce—laws, constitutions, religions, poetry—always is, in a way, a collective work, the result of a union of all faculties and forces.

This was the fourth great mother-idea, if I may so call it, that gave birth to the German view of mind and nature, man and history, which ' we have proposed to examine. We have now to ₋ see what became of the seeds of thought sown in Germany between 1760 and 1770 by the hands of the four great geniuses who are to be considered as the real architects of our culture. We shall try to form to ourselves an idea of Herder's own view on mankind and history in his maturer age, of Goethe's view on mankind and nature, Kant's view on mankind and morality, Schiller's view on mankind and art.

LECTURE IV.

WE have seen that the principal ideas which
Germany had to develop and illustrate in her
national literature and in her scientific work were
almost all thrown on the intellectual market of
Europe shortly after the conclusion of the Seven
Years' War. Winckelmann gave new life to antiquity by applying to it a new historical method.
Lessing traced the limits between the fine arts and
poetry, assigning to each of them a domain not
to be overstepped. Kant, correcting Rousseau's
view of the history of mankind, contended that the
ideal aim of mankind was not the natural state of
the savage as Rousseau held, but a state of nature
combined with intellectual, moral, æsthetic, and
political development, such as was realised in
Greece. Herder, finally, starting likewise from

Rousseau, believed all great creations of humanity to be the work of spontaneous action, either individual or collective and national, not the intentional result of self-conscious activity. The three first of these four great men still belong to the generation of 1760, as we should call the men born in the second and third decade of the century; the last, Herder, born in 1744, already belongs to the following generation, that of Goethe. His marvellous precocity alone permitted him to fight at the side of Lessing, his elder by fifteen years.

It seems natural that the youngest of the prophets should also be the one most eagerly listened to by the youth of his country; it becomes more natural when we take into account the inspired and inspiring personality of the man who at twenty-two stirred the German world by his apparent paradoxes, who at twenty-six was the Mentor, the initiator, the guiding genius of Goethe, his junior only by five years. And not of Goethe alone, although his personal relations with him were more intimate than with others, but of the whole generation of 1775. It is not too much to say that he inspired all the writers of this period of literary history—and Germany had then scarcely any but literary history—the *Sturm- und Drang-*

periode, which lasted from about 1770 till about
1786. Herder, it is true, gave to his thoughts
their lasting and determined form only in 1784,
when he published his principal work, the 'Ideas
on a Philosophy of the History of Mankind.'
This great book, however, only develops the conceptions which were in the germ in the 'Fragments,' the 'Critical Sylvæ,' and the 'Origin of
Language,' just as in the 'Letters on the Study
of Theology' and the 'Spirit of Hebrew Poetry'
(1781–1782) we find the very thoughts which he
had laid before the public ten years earlier in his
'Most Ancient Document of Humanity'—thoughts
which opened quite a new insight into the secret
laboratory of language, poetry, and religion.
Even the memorable book, which has been father
to all the histories of poetry, religion, language
and law of our century—even the 'Ideas'—are
unfinished, diffusely written in a loose disconnected
style, the style of a seer rather than of a thinker,
and still less that of an historian; very insufficient if we look upon them as a collection of researches, nay, totally antiquated as
far as form and materials are concerned. But
as for the thoughts contained in it, the book
seems written but yesterday; it might easily

be taken for a sketch from the pen of M.
Taine.

The one chief conception, we have seen, which
Herder sought to impress on his age, was that of
Herder's   evolution, growth, *fieri*, which he had
views.   borrowed from the vegetable kingdom in
order to apply it to political, religious, and literary
history; nay, to the natural history of man and to
that of his language.

He, and Hamann before him, had been struck
by the little help obtained from isolated observation
towards arriving at the truth. They saw that
almost all our knowledge is acquired by synthetic
and unconscious observation, or, to use a more accu-
rate term, reception; while intuition—*i.e.* the spark
which suddenly shows the link and coherence of
such synthetic knowledge, and which is after all
only the result of long unconscious reception and
unconscious maturation of what has been received
—seemed to them infinitely superior to consciously
generalising and arguing reason, which had been
so exclusively used in their century. Hence their
two leading ideas, which gradually acquired depth,
width, and strength, became the two leading ideas
of German culture: the first being that of the
totality of individual or collective forces as opposed

to the division of labour; the second, that of the
unintentional origin of all great individual and
collective creations.

Now the unconscious creative power, working
in man and nature, manifests itself nowhere so
strikingly as in *genius*—the genius not only of the
great legislator, captain, philosopher, poet, but also
the genius of naïveté, *i.e.* of any single human
being, or collection of human beings, not yet
affected by our abstract and analytical habits.

Our minds to day are differently framed from those of
primitive men, owing to the education of our youth for so
many past generations. We are accustomed to reflect
and analyse so much that we hardly see or feel any more.
We no longer poetise in or on the living world; our
poetry is not the result of the contact of objects with our
soul; we manufacture artificially both the subjects and
the modes of treating them; and we have practised this so
long and so frequently, and we begin to do so at so early
an age, that a free education would have small chance of
success with us; for how should the lame learn to walk
upright?

The starting-point, then, of Herder's whole
philosophy is the conception of genius as the one
acting force of the intellectual world. 'What is
it in Homer that compensates for his ignorance of
the rules, deduced from the study of his works by

Aristotle? What in Shakespeare that makes up
for his direct violation even of these laws of criticism? The unanimous answer to the question
will be : Genius.' These words of Hamann may
be considered as the theme of all Herder's variations. Now, the nature of *genius* consists in the
elementary operations of the mind before habits
of analysis and abstraction have severed the different mental faculties and have accustomed man to
form general conceptions and to influence his will
by them. Its essence is direct sensation and intuition, unconscious production. It lives principally in popular poetry, legislation, and religion,
not yet influenced by rationalistic culture. Even
nowadays it cannot survive unless it keeps itself
free from all rationalistic rules, and obeys only
its inspiration. We shall see by and by to what
errors this principle led us soon as it was applied
to science, which rests entirely on the combination
of observation and reasoning; and to morals, the
very essence of which is connected in our own
minds with the idea of duty. Let us confine ourselves for the moment to poetry and history in the
widest sense, comprising theology, philology, &c.,
where this point of view was exceedingly fertile
and salutary.

Indeed, the much vaunted originality not being of frequent occurrence in the eminently artificial society of the eighteenth century, it be- On Poetry. came necessary, in order to find it in all its purity, either to ascend to epochs which preceded civilisation—in other words, to primitive nations, —or to descend to those popular strata of the existing age which had as yet escaped the contagion of corrupt culture.   Herder, you see, was a kind of literary Rousseau.   He may be said to have renovated and regenerated the poetry of his time by immersing it in the true sources of all great poetry : nature and popular life.   He it was who first established the fact, subsequently confirmed by historical discovery, that poetry always pre- ceded prose in the annals of mankind ; he it was who first proclaimed the poetical superiority of ages in which the entireness of individuality was not yet broken.

In the flourishing periods of elegant prose, he would say, nothing but art can prosper in poetry.   Later on we find even mere versified philosophy and half-way poetry. On the other hand, the language of those times, when words had not yet been divided into nobles, middle-class, and plebeians, nor had prose been sifted, was the richest for poetical purposes.   Our tongue compared with the idiom of the savage seems adapted rather for reflection

than for the senses or imagination. The rhythm of popular
verse is so delicate, so rapid, so precise, that it is no easy
matter for us bookworms to detect it with our eyes; but
do not imagine it to have been equally difficult for those
living populations who listened to, instead of reading it;
who were accustomed to the sound of it from their infancy;
who themselves sang it, and whose ear had been formed
by its cadence.

And here Herder enters into one of the topics
which he has made so wonderfully his own—that
of the organ of the ear—but it would lead me too
far if I were to quote *in extenso*.   Suffice it to say
that his essentially musical nature made him particularly apt to listen to that innermost life of the
soul, which can be expressed only by tone and
rhythm.   If he so continually and persistently
contemplates primitive ages, and incessantly op-
poses them to his own conventional age, it is
chiefly because that innermost life was more
intense then, because thoughts, facts, images even
of primitive man had not yet been severed from
this innermost life, and consequently still wanted
the help of music, as the only adequate language
of it, in order to give them expression.

Poetry in those happy days lived in the ears of the
people, on the lips and in the harps of living bards; it

sang of history, of the events of the day, of mysteries, miracles, and signs. It was the flower of a nation's character, language, and country; of its occupations, its prejudices, its passions, its aspirations, and its soul.

The whole modern theory concerning epic poetry is contained in embryo in these words. Yet Herder goes still further, and formulates it so distinctly that F. A. Wolf had scarcely anything to do but to develop and establish it more firmly by means of that detailed and solid system of argumentation, which made him the true father of the Homeric idea, as comprehended by our age.

The greatest among Greek bards was also the greatest among popular poets. His sublime work is no epopœia; it is the *epos*, the story, the legend, the living history of the people. He did not sit down on velvet cushions to compose a poem in twice twenty-four cantos according to the rules of Aristotle.

Words like these naturally fell like thunderbolts on that eighteenth century, so self-satisfied, so vain of the great progress it had achieved and of the high culture it had attained. Versification as an art had been brought to such perfection, the criterion by which the merits and demerits of poetry were to be measured had been so accurately defined, poetry itself was so easily learnt and

taught, that the world was completely dumb-
foundered at this strange enthusiasm for miserable,
despised savages. Moreover, Herder added practice
to theory.   During his stay at Strassburg, he
had already begun with Goethe to search for
popular songs, and great was his delight when he
was able to send one to his affianced bride, which
he had gathered from the mouth of the people.
No book, since the appearance of Percy's ' Relics,'
had met with such success in Germany as the
' Voices of Nations,' a series of volumes containing
popular poems in masterly translations, and published by Herder in 1778.   It became indeed the
model for all the numerous collections of the
kind which have come out during the nineteenth
century.

But Herder not only discovered true living
poetry in the distant ages of Homer and the
cloudy isles of Ossian; he found it out in modern
times, in his own nation, lending a ready ear to
the simple ditties of the woodcutter and the
peasant, of the journeyman and the soldier, of the
hunter and the shepherd.   Germany owes the
revival of the *lied* or song entirely to Herder and
to his ' Stimmen der Völker.'   When we read the
verses which Goethe wrote at Leipzig, before

meeting with Herder, we may well be permitted to
doubt whether Germany would have ever possessed
those unrivalled pearls, his little songs of love, addressed to Friederike and Lili, if he had not known
him. It is, at any rate, very doubtful whether it
would have had the ' Erlkönig ' or the ' Fisherman.'
Of these, however, England possesses beautiful
examples in her own ballads; not so of the *lied*,
with which even Burns's poems have little in
common, and of which we find only the *pendant* in
Shakespeare's little songs, such as—

> Blow, blow, thou winter wind !

and others.

It is difficult indeed to define the *lied*.

What is the *lied* ? Herder asked. It is neither a
sonnet nor a madrigal, poems for the study and the salon ;
it is no composition for painting with harmonious colouring ; light and brilliancy are not its merits. . . . The
essence of the *lied* is *song*, not painting. Its perfection
resides in the melodious course of a passion or a
sentiment. . . . If this melody be wanting in a *lied*, if it
have not the poetical modulation, the right tone, it may
contain ever so many images, it may be graceful, it may
have colouring ; it never can be a *lied*.

And as with the epic poem, the ballad, and the
lied, so with the fable. Lafontaine had made

delicious *tableaux de genre* of the fable of the
ancients; Lessing concise, epigrammatic satires.
Nay, Lessing had still defined the fable in the
spirit of the eighteenth century as an intentional
form of moral teaching: 'If we reduce a general
proposition to a particular case, lending it reality
and making a story out of it,.in which the general
proposition may be recognised by means of intuition, we call this a fable.' How much deeper
is Herder's view. In his eyes fables originally
were, and would again become, were we to live
less artificially, the ' poetical illustration of a
lesson of experience by means of a characteristic
trait, drawn from animal life and developed by
analogy.'

In ancient fables (he says) animals act, because whatever in nature produces effects appears to primitive
humanity to act. . . . It is analogy which is the parent
of poetry in fables, not abstraction, still less a dry deduc-
tion from the general to the particular. . . . The fable
rests on Nature's eternal consistency and constancy. . . .
Its characters are types. . . . The more natural the state
in which a nation lived, the more it liked fables.

·Now, Herder made this refutation of the
mechanical theories, then reigning throughout
Europe, from his point of view, *i.e.* that of spon-

taneous creation without special conscious aim, not
only in the domain of the fable, but in that of every
kind of poetry. He carefully studied the nature of
the epigram in its earliest form, and of _{On Anti-}
the national drama, as he had studied _{quity.}
that of the *lied* and the epic poem, chiefly illus-
trating his theories from Greek examples. The
whole of the ancient world has been looked upon
with different eyes since Herder. Viewing the
ancients as an historian alone could view them, he
opposed his own less refined conception of antiquity,
not only to the Alexandrian, rather than the Athe-
nian, conventional antiquity which found favour
with the French and Wieland, but also indirectly
and half-unconsciously to Winckelmann's somewhat cothurnic idealism. For him the first, Achilles
and Ajax became chiefs of clans, instead of princes
of the blood, or lords of a royal court *à la* Versailles,
as Apollo and Diana became living mythical
figures instead of cold allegories. It was Herder
who taught young Goethe to laugh at Wieland's
powdered and patched Alcestis in his charming
satire, ' Gods, heroes, and Wieland ' (1774), as it
was Herder who made him understand the beauty
of the Strassburg Cathedral, then considered as a
work of barbarism, and express in his Essay on

K

'German Architecture' those simple and profound thoughts on art, which ought to have put a stop to all our systematic imitations of past and foreign styles which correspond to nothing in our life.

Herder's views, however, failed unfortunately to prevail within the province of plastic art, owing to the powerful and yet too recent influence and authority exercised by Winckelmann. But they penetrated rapidly into all other branches of intellectual activity in Germany; into historical studies particularly, for Herder himself applied his main conception of poetry to the history of states, civil law, and religions. It is true he placed the history of civilisation far above political history. Still he included political history in that of civilisation, and thereby he made a real revolution in historical science, or I had perhaps better say in the art of history. Up to his time the most mechanical teleology had reigned in the philosophy of history. Providence was represented to have created 'cork-trees that men should have wherewithal to stop their bottles;' as also, of course, to have prevented Cromwell from setting out for America in order that an instrument might not be wanting to ac-

On His-
tory.

complish the Revolution in England. Bossuet's *Discours sur l'histoire universelle* is still entirely based upon the programme-idea ; and Montesquieu, in his *Grandeur et décadence,* if he does not bring in the Divine *régisseur,* lends to the mortal actors of history plans and intentions, and ascribes to laws and institutions an influence which they never had. Herder was the first who ventured to leave the alleged aims of Providence as well as those of theoretical legislation in historical events out of the question, and opposing himself alike to the idea of a preconceived plan, and that of mere chance, refused to see anything in history beyond the development of given germs. This has undoubtedly proved the most fertile of modern ideas. 'Each nation contains its centre within itself, as a bullet its centre of gravity. There is nothing within the whole kingdom of God which is a mere means ; everything is at once means and end.' He was the first also to banish the conscious legislators out of primitive history. For him Lycurgus was already what Otfried Müller proved him to be fifty years later, the legendary judge who, according to tradition, codified the secular uses and customs of his tribe, not the inventor of a brand new constitution planned *ad hoc* like that of the Abbé Sieyès. The

K 2

pervading spirit of his great book is a sort of warfare against mechanical causes or abstract ideas, introduced as realities into history, and above all against teleology, which looks for an end or purpose in every event. The historian, he says, 'will never attempt to explain a thing which *is* by a thing which *is not.* And with this severe principle all ideals, all phantasmas of a dream-world disappear.' Consequently we must beware of referring the phenomena of history to a design or plan which is unknown to us. To the question, 'Why did Alexander go to India?' there is only one answer, 'Because he was Alexander, Philip's son.' In giving up this investigation into a plan of history we are recompensed by getting an insight into the high and beautiful laws of nature. Indeed,

'. . . if there is a God in nature, he is also in history; for man is also part of the creation, and must, even in his wildest excesses and passions, obey laws, which are no less beautiful and excellent than those according to which all the celestial bodies move.' . . . 'The God I look for in history must be the same as the God of nature; for man is but a tiny particle of the whole, and the *history of mankind resembles that of the worm, closely connected with the tissue it inhabits*; therefore the natural laws by which the Deity reveals itself must reign in man likewise.' And elsewhere: '. . . The whole history of humanity is pure natural history of human forces, actions, and instincts. according to place and time.'

This is the view of human history which we shall afterwards see Goethe applying to nature, nor can the resemblance surprise any one who knows how intimately the two men lived together. Herder has not only a wonderful insight into the early periods of history—one must read his diary during his journey from Riga to Nantes to see how the mystery of the formation of States, and of the migration and settlements of nations, revealed itself to him—he has even profound views on the prehistoric state of mankind which belongs still, up to a certain point, to natural history. And a great naturalist of our days (Baer) could say of him that he 'had drawn with the divination of a seer the outlines of comparative anatomy of which the works of Cuvier and our time give only the commentary.' Now, Herder's principle as applied to historic as well as prehistoric times, is that everywhere on earth all beings become what they can become according to the situation and necessities of place, according to the circumstances and opportunities of time, and according to the inborn or acquired physical and intellectual character of the race; in other words, M. Taine's

'*milieu, moment, et race.*' No doubt, Montesquieu in his famous seventeenth and eighteenth
books had already given great importance to the
influence of climate and soil on the destinies
of nations; but he, wisely enough, made of them
only contributing elements, and although his
views on this matter taken in themselves may be
sounder than those of Herder, it is certain that
they have not acted on the general current of
thought as Herder's did, perhaps also because he
exposed them less persistently and less enthusiastically.

The plan which Herder proposed to the future
historian was to take his start from the Universum,
marking the position of the earth in it, and to
show the condition of life on earth, resulting from
this position; then to describe the typical forms
of plants and animals ' until the physiogromy of
the earth as a whole should be entirely grasped
with all the conditions it offers for human history.'
The great geographical work of K. Ritter, who
wrote these words, as well as those of A. von Humboldt, are the fruit of this method recommended
by Herder. All this, however, was for him only
the basis of a History of Man.

Man is the last and highest link in the development of the creating power, which lives in the earth. He shows how the progress of nature produced a more and more refined brain until it arrived at man. The same organic evolution which gave him the most developed brain gave him also language. Indeed, whilst one-half of the cultivated world still saw in language a gift or revelation of God, the other an intentional, human invention, Herder already saw in it, what we all nowadays see in it, a potential instrument for the development of reason, a natural product of the soul's vital forces, an ever self-creating process. For it is through language that we must understand the birth of abstract reason, i.e. the faculty of forming general conceptions, which is not a primitive faculty, common to all men from the beginning, but one acquired by the co-operation of language and intelligence.

According to Herder's conception of organic development, therefore, the human alone can be the ideal aim of mankind. A morality, which affects anything higher, would be a delusion.

If we examine mankind—if we look on mankind, as we know it to be, i.e. according to the laws which are within it—we know nothing higher than humanity in man. Even when we imagine angels and gods, we imagine them as ideal, higher men.

The Deity has limited man's possibilities only
by time, place, and innate faculties. The one
active force is the creative power of man's nature,
which the environment hinders or furthers more
or less. Now, the law of this progress and development is, that all destructive forces must, in the
long run, not only succumb to the conservative
forces, but also serve to the development of the
whole. This the history of the animal kingdom
shows as well as the history of mankind.[1]

Though Herder is continually appealing to
God, all this sounds singularly like pantheism,
On Reli- and the words which I have quoted are
gion. not such as he would. have penned at
Bückeburg at the time he made the first rough
sketch of his philosophy of history. But, since
then, he, like Lessing, Goethe, and nearly all the
eminent minds of the age, had tasted of Spinoza
and relished him extremely. In spite of the
scandal produced among believers by this change,
Herder never renounced his new faith, even after
having attained the highest ecclesiastical dignities.
He sought to conceal it, more certainly from himself than from others, and in order to do this he

[1] See the 'Ideas' *passim*, and particularly Book xv. 1 and 2
Cf. Book xiii. 7, on Greek history in general.

was obliged to put much into Christianity which
does not really belong to it, as many others before
and since have done.

The pearl is found (he says) ; no one can build upon
any other foundation than that of Christ. As this Gospel
needs no external signs, being its own proof, neither can
it be overthrown by theological or other doubts. . . . In
all the things which occur in the world, it is its kingdom
which is coming ; for this is the business of Providence,
and it is the aim and character, the very essence of the
human race to accomplish the work of Providence. Put
no trust in phantoms. The kingdom of God is within you.

This religion, you see, was a very wide one,
and this species of Christianity very closely re-
sembled the doctrines of Spinoza. But it was
precisely in virtue of the peculiar wideness of his
Christianity that Herder exercised so great an
influence over his country. If the German people
has been—till lately, at least—the only one
which has remained deeply religious without
paying any great attention to external worship,
religious observance and dogmas, it has merely
followed the example which Herder gave it.

The question has been raised whether a man can be
moral independently of religion—independently of religious dogma is undoubtedly what is meant, for other-

wise this question would be resolved by itself. True religion cannot exist without morality, and true morality is religion under whatever form it may show itself.

This, translated into Luther's language, means that faith goes before works: the man who lives in the ideal cannot be immoral, the modern German would say, in accordance therein with the unconscious belief of all his forefathers. As far from orthodoxy as from rationalism, Herder constantly appeals from dogma and reasoning to religious feeling: 'Flee religious controversy as you would the plague,' he used to say, 'for it is impossible to dispute about what religion is. It is as impossible either to deny or affirm it by discussion as to paint the mind or hear light.' It is precisely because Christianity is an especially human religion that Herder feels himself a Christian; for the development of the human was the ideal of his life. The natural nobility of man was great enough in his eyes without claiming a supranatural one for him.

Herder's religious development is very characteristic of Germany in the past century. The Bible was for him the earliest source of intellectual culture, as it was for Klopstock, Lessing, and above all Goethe. At an early age, however, he rebels

against the idea of its being a revealed book.
Genesis became in his eyes only a kind of theo-
gony, like that of Hesiod, nor could he see anything
beyond a collection of national chronicles, poems
and proverbs, in the rest of the Old Testament.
What he discovers in it above all is poetry; and
we find him defending the Song of Solomon as
energetically against mystics as against moralising
rationalists. It is necessary to read his eloquent
pages on the Mosaic epopœia in order to understand the effect which they produced in their
apparently profane treatment of the subject. For
Herder, of course, and his countrymen it was only
another form of admiration. 'Burn all rationalistic metaphysics!' he exclaims. 'The living
commentary on the Mosaic monument blows
with the morning air.' Herder it was who first
taught the world to understand the Oriental way
of thinking, who first showed it what Oriental
poetry was, and opposed the primitive simplicity
of the Bible to the dogmatic interpretation of
theologians. And he finds beautiful words to
praise the beauty of this Oriental poetry of the
Bible.

These ideas Herder brought forward for the
first time in his 'Most Ancient Document,' which

he 'had cherished in his heart from his tenderest infancy.' They were taken up again and developed still further eight and ten years later in his ' Letters on the Study of Theology,' and in the ' Spirit of Hebrew Poetry.' He never tires of telling the world that the Bible is not only the basis of our own religion, but also contains that which is the most elevated and ancient in the world. (At that time the Vedas had not yet been discovered.) It was he above all who opened the world's eyes anew to that poetry which had been hidden from its sight by the mass of allegory, morals, dogmas, philosophical ideas, and law texts with which it had been stifled. For he had the boldness to treat the Bible like any other human document; and by doing so, he rendered possible the history of religion which belongs essentially and exclusively to our age. For nothing less than the example of Herder's deep and sincere religious feeling would have sufficed to enable men of those times to study religion itself without placing themselves at the point of view of any given religion. The various forms under which mankind have successively or simultaneously tried to satisfy their craving for the infinite and the supernatural, had to be duly respected and loved; but it was needful also to reach the point at which the believer no longer requires that the infinite and supernatural should have a definite and conventional form, in order to adore and dread it. An enthusiastic nature was needed, like that of Herder, capable of understanding a mystical glow, and yet free-thinking enough not to attribute to himself and his sect alone the privilege of such mystical glow and the immediate conception of the Deity. The Tübingen school would have been an impossibility without Herder, and we may say exactly the same thing with regard to its adversaries. Ewald would never have written his 'History of the People of Israel;' Bunsen would never have composed his great 'Bible-work,' nor his 'God in History,' if Herder had not opened out fresh horizons to theology and history. Even E. Renan finds himself still upon ground which Herder has conquered for religious history. Respect and sympathy for religion are here allied to an independence of view which regards all religions as issuing from the same religious want, and which substitutes internal for external revelation.

Herder no longer explains the origin of positive religion, as it was customary to do in the philosophical camp, by the imposture of priests,

but historically. First he sees fear and superstition; then curiosity, creating cosmogonies, and,
with the aid of poetical imagination, mythology.
He shows that religious ideas become simplified,
generalised, and purified only by degrees. In
the beginning they could only be instinctive,
intuitive, sensuous, and consequently local and
definite.

It was natural that these traditions should be more
national than anything else in the world. Everyone
spoke through the mouth of his forefathers, saw by the
standard of the world which surrounded him; gave himself solutions concerning the problems which interested
him most, such as were best adapted to his climate,
nationality, and traditions. . . . Scandinavia built a world
of giants; the Iroquois made the turtle the machine
which explained to him the existence of the earth.

The whole of modern religious criticism, its
fertility as well as its perils, is contained in these
words. For how should a grosser mind, or simply
a less poetical, less respectful soul than Herder's,
translate all this otherwise than by the well-known
words of the arch-scoffer: 'God created man after
his own image and man gave it him back?' Nor
are gross minds, cold and irreverent souls less
common among the defenders than among the

detractors of positive religion. Warburton would
not have understood Herder better than he was
understood by Paine. Hence the great unpopu-
larity of Herder and his disciples in both camps.

It is usual to call Herder the apostle of
humanitarian ideas, and not without reason, provided a contempt for nationalities be not   On
implied. Herder, like Lessing, who de-   Humanity.
clared patriotism to be a virtue of doubtful worth,
like Goethe, like Schiller above all, placed humanity higher than nationality. In his eyes the title
' man ' was the noblest which could be imagined,
and he still belongs entirely to his essentially
optimistic century by this very exalted idea of man.
In his eyes national prejudices were as contempt-
ible as were religious and caste prejudices. He
thought that a day would come when a single
bond would unite all peoples, when a single, un-
written religion, a single civilisation, a single
morality would bring men together in a common
brotherhood. He protested vehemently against
national exclusiveness, as he protested against
every other species of exclusiveness. He did not
wish that any people, not even his own, should be
trumpeted forth as the elect; but he was not the
less full of love and reverence for his country on

that account, and I may anticipate what I shall
have to say later, by stating that this spirit of
temperate patriotism, which desires for our native
country an equal, but never a predominant, place
among nations, has given the main impulse to
the national revival of Germany in this century,
and still moves and sways the mass as well as
the *élite* of the nation.

National pride (said Herder) is absurd, ridiculous,
and dangerous; but it is everybody's duty to love his
country, and it cannot be loved if it is not honoured, or if
it is allowed to be disparaged. It must be defended, and
each of us must contribute the utmost in his power to its
honour and welfare.

Far from being a despiser of his own country,
Herder was perhaps the most patriotic German
writer of the last century, although he had not
continuously 'Hermann, the Cherusk,' and the
'Roman tyrants' in his mouth like Klopstock and
the Stolbergs. He was undoubtedly the one who
best understood the degradation and who most
deplored the fragmentary condition, the slavery
and political *décadence* of the Empire. He laments
that Germany was but 'a thing of the imagination,'
that she had no 'common voice,' that there was
no **Frederick II.** seated upon the worm-eaten

throne of the German Cæsars. And as, in opposition to Schiller, he desired that poetry should seek her inspiration in real life and not in the ideal world, he likewise wished, in opposition to Goethe, that this reality should be that of public, not for ever that of private, life. In particular his 'Letters on Humanity,' especially the first, are full of these patriotic and political ideas. But it would convey a false impression if I did not add that in his eyes the nation was but ' a member of humankind.' His demand was that nations should exercise a mutual influence over each other by means of their moral and intellectual qualities only, and he saw in a ' free competition of activity among the different nationalities the fundamental condition of the civilisation of mankind.' Certainly it seems to have been his mission to preach the Human, but also to show it in all its manifold forms. For he contended even against Lessing that human development is conditioned by nationality and natural surroundings, that in the vicissitudes of history the ideal of the Human never appears nor ever will appear in one universal form.

This man it is who, thanks to some ill-comprehended sentence of a speech made in his youth, has become the ' apostle of cosmopolitism '

L

in the eyes of posterity. One ought far rather to say that, after having been the standard-bearer in the revolt of the Teutonic against the Latin spirit by his literary criticism, he was at once the first and the most eloquent defender of that principle of nationalities which has agitated our own century so deeply. By restoring national poetry to its place of honour he contributed indirectly to the revival of patriotic sentiments ; by formulating *the* German idea he became the forerunner of those who, long after, created the German State.

As for himself, Herder was a citizen of all countries and ages, as he was a reader of all literatures. He deemed it necessary to know and appreciate the poetry of other countries as well as of his own ; and to be able to do this properly it was indispensable that he should place himself amongst the surroundings which had produced it. Now, nature had endowed him for this purpose with a pliability of intelligence, an acuteness of perception, a keenness of sight and hearing, a refined delicacy of taste totally unrivalled. This faculty of appreciating and entering into the spirit of the most divers countries and periods constitutes his chief and true grandeur, and he bequeathed a good part of it to the culture of Germany. This was in reality his cosmopolitism, which has been so often

misrepresented, and about which a legion of historians have been content to repeat stereotyped
judgments, without attempting to subject them to
the slightest criticism. This cosmopolitism never
for a moment prevented him from being the most
German of all German writers in the general tone
of his inspiration, still less from heralding the
German idea to the world with that exaggeration
which is always to be found in reactions, and which
it is the task of our time to moderate.

In fact, as we have seen, Herder not only put
an end to the remnants of reasoning, didactics,
and moralising which even Lessing had still
admitted into the domain of poetry; he combated
them also in the field of religion, politics, and
historical science, as he also rose up against the
idea of *rule* which Lessing defended, for the essentially German conception of individual right.   He
restored originality, if I may say so, to German
poetry and thought by setting limits for a while
to the imitation of the ancients ; and the form and
spirit of his teaching were eminently German.
For, although Germany has had more than one
matter-of-fact and sober genius since Luther, still
Herder's rather musical than plastic genius, his
high-flown, enthusiastic nature, his want of measure

and of definiteness, his wonderful intuitive power, his rather unmethodical reasoning, and his faculty of 'assimilation are, after all, more characteristic of the German nature than the practical sense and the energy of a Frederick and a Bismarck, the dialectical prowess of a. Lessing, or the plastic power of a Goethe.

There was one quality besides, almost lost, it seemed, since the days of Leibnitz, which Herder restored to his nation and bequeathed to its civilisation and thought : universality and breadth of horizon. Understanding nationality as few persons of his time understood it, he subordinated it to humanity. Brought up in reverence for Hellenism, and the first to point out its true character, he discovered the East by intuition. In heart a Christian, he knew how to assimilate all the 'pagan' humanism of the Renaissance. Full of admiration for the classical authors, he found the secret of primitive and religious poetry. Liberal in his political sympathies, he demonstrated the laws and consistency of history. No manifestation of mankind, whatever its form, had a secret for the apostle of humanity.

The movement initiated by Herder was a general one, and it extended from Königsberg to Zürich, from Strassburg to Dresden, every town of Germany taking part in it, more or less. Not only universities and *Sturm- und Drang- periode.* republics, like Göttingen and Frankfort, but small capitals also, such as Darmstadt, Weimar, Stuttgart, saw the 'geniuses' hurl their clamorous challenge and defy the heaven in their desire to renew and regenerate the world by a return to Nature; for the young disciples, as disciples *will* do, began forthwith to out-Herder Herder. The preceding generation had been concentrating its powers for action, and Berlin had been Lessing's headquarters. Young Germany of 1775 overflowed the entire country, finding voluntary agents and apostles in all quarters. The same ideas which Hamann had instilled into Herder, when on the shores of the Baltic, were to strike his ear as soon as he approached Switzerland, where Lavater was preaching them with still greater zeal and in more whimsical language than the 'Magician of the North.'

When a student at Königsberg, indeed, Herder had undergone not only Kant's influence, but also, and still more, Hamann's. He *Königs- berg.*

owed to Kant—not yet the man who wrote the
Critic of Pure Reason, and opened new horizons
to man's intelligence—the awakening of his philosophical thought.

I once had the happiness of knowing a philosopher; he
was my teacher. He had the joyous cheerfulness of
youth at that happy time; his open forehead, created ex-
pressly for thought, was the seat of imperturbable serenity;
his speech, redundant with ideas, flowed from his lips; he
always had some humorous *trait*, some witty sally at his
disposal: . . . He would constantly bring us back to the
simple, unaffected study of nature. . . . He gave me self-
confidence, and obliged me to think for myself, for tyranny
was foreign to his soul.

And Kant himself, on reading some verses of the
enthusiastic boy, said: 'When this boiling genius
has done fermenting, he will be a very useful man.'
Who could then have predicted the desperate
warfare which was to break out between these
two great men thirty years later? Even then,
however, it was Hamann's more than Kant's
merit to have shown Herder the road he was to
follow. Hamann is not to be counted among the
German classical writers, although he left several
volumes; for all he produced was of a fragmentary nature. He abounded in new and original
ideas, but there were as many 'nebulous spots as

stars on that firmament' (Jean Paul), and the dis-
order of his brain was as clearly reflected in his
'grasshopper-style' as it was in his odd person.
This singularly active power—Goethe called him
'the indispensable, but indigestible leaven' of
the time—must in a great measure, of course,
escape the scrutiny of history; nor is it easy to
explain it otherwise than by the persistency with
which Hamann harped upon that fundamental
theme then about to become the leading principle
of the generation : the theme of absolute individual
liberty. He excited Herder against the dead letter
of poetical rule, as well as against the narrow-
minded morality of the middle classes. He was
as rebellious against the 'modern State' of the
Philosopher King, as against 'enlightenment'
and rationalism in religion ; but it was reserved
to the disciple to set the 'unstrung pearls' of
the Königsberg 'Magus.'

The University of Göttingen was a still more
agitated centre of movement than that of Königsberg. There Bürger had just written his
'Lenore,' and those other early ballads
Göttingen.
which at once took Germany by storm ; there some
young students had formed among themselves a
poetical league, which assembled around the secu-

lar oaks of the neighbouring forest, invoking the
memory of Hermann, the liberator, and the Teutonic bards, worshipping Klopstock, and burning
Wieland's works. The famous 'Hainbund' num-
bered among its associates many celebrated names.
There were the two impetuous Counts Stolberg, the
'enemies of tyrants'—dead tyrants, of course—
Voss, the peasant-boy and future poet of 'Louise,'
he who gave Germany what Heine called the *Vul-
gate* of Homer, and who, forty years later, declared
war upon Fritz Stolberg, when this friend of his
youth fled into the arms of Rome; his brother-in-
law, Boie, who published the first poetical alma-
nack, the 'Moniteur' of the League; melancholy
Hölty, doomed to early death, and many other
poets who afterwards got a high reputation, but
the eldest of whom at that time was hardly
twenty-two years of age; sincere and pure and
high-minded youths all of them, but somewhat intentional in their enthusiasm, not without unconscious affectation beneath the surface of their mag-
niloquent vehemence; more bent upon looking for
the poetical in abstract thought and vague feelings
than in sensuous reality and its definite forms.

In the South, especially in Würtemberg, a soil
which has always been productive of revolutionary

radicalism, it was no longer rebellion against
literary authority alone which armed the Würtem-
poets. They did not limit themselves berg.
to ridiculing, like Bürger, 'Mam'zell la Règle,
nursery-governess and duenna, half French, half
Greek, ever ready to watch over the children of
the German Muse, preventing them from straying
on to the flower-beds and admonishing them to
hold up their heads, turn out their toes, and
stretch their arms.' Here it was not only against
the yoke of scholastic pedantry in science and
thought that protest was made, as in the North ;
here was not only a platonic hatred vowed against
religious and political oppression, as in the plains
of Göttingen ; here there was rebellion against
the established authorities as well. Despotism had
put such a strain upon the springs in the little
country of Suabia that at last they threatened to
snap asunder. The worship of Rousseau nowhere
found more numerous and more fervent adherents than in the native land of Schiller. The
young writer of the 'Brigands' had himself much
to bear from the intolerable yoke of 'Denys
turned into a schoolmaster.' It is well known
how he escaped from the Duke's College by flight,
and what eloquent, clamorous protest he hurled

from that time against despotism in ' Fiesco,' in
' Cabal and Love,' in ' Don Carlos.' His gipsy-
like countryman Weckherlin, who protested in his
newspapers, divided his life between prison and
exile. Before him Schubart, the journalist, scholar,
musician and poet, the model and ideal of Schiller's
early days, had raised his voice in impetuous
stanzas, and expiated the temerity of his ' Fürsten-
gruft ' by ten years of solitary captivity in the
famous castle of Hohenasperg, which received
within its walls many other high-minded men,
determined to resist absolute rule.

More to the South still, in the old Swiss republics, ' preserved in spirits of wine,' as Goethe

Zürich.

used to say, the new ideas also worked
against the antiquated and petrified forms
of state, society, religion. There it was that
Pestalozzi, inflamed by Rousseau's ' Emile,' attempted to elevate the lower classes by a more
natural education, without falling into the ex-
tremes of the other great school reformer of the
day, Basedow, who had also waged war against
all the traditional systems. Basedow, however,
who was one of Goëthe's odd travelling companions
on the Rhine,[1] preached and worked mostly in the

---

[1] Prophete rechts, Prophete links,
Das Weltkind in der Mitten.

north of Germany. The other 'prophet,' Lavater (born 1741), the famous physiognomist, taught the new religion in Zürich, which ever since the beginning of the century had been an active focus of literary life. Reviving pietism in a way by giving it a sort of poetical colour and combining with it a high culture, little familiar to the humble brethren, he pretended to regenerate Christianity by the inner light, by the revelation every day repeated. With the tone of an inspired seer he boasted of having found again the Divine word, which had been lost. In his heart he felt Christ born anew. This tone and these ideas he brought also into the poetical domain where he would recognise genius alone. Young Goethe was content to proclaim the autocracy of Genius, which ' school could but fetter,' and to which ' principles were more noxious even than examples ; ' Lavater went the length of actual worship :

Geniuses (he would exclaim), lights of the world, salt of the earth, nouns in the grammar of humanity, images of Deity, human Gods, creators, destroyers, revealers of the secrets of God and man, drogmans of nature, prophets, priests, kings of the world—it is of you I speak, it is you 1 ask, How did the Deity call you ?

There you have something of the reigning

hero- worship in its abstrusest form ; and, of course, among the worshipped heroes was the prophet himself and even his disciples. Nothing could give a better idea of the ways and spirit of this strange young generation than these bizarre effusions. However tedious may be the tortured style of the enthusiast, one must endure it if we would understand the time.

The character of genius is apparition, which, like that of an angel, does not come, but is there, which, like that, strikes the innermost marrow . . . and disappears and continues acting after having disappeared, and leaves behind itself sweet shudders and tears of terror and paleness of joy which are the work and effect of genius. Call it as thou likest—call it fecundity of mind, inexhaustibility, unequalled strength, primitive force, elasticity of soul, call it central spirit, central fire, or simply invention, instinct, the not-learned, the not-borrowed, the unlearnable, the unborrowable, etc , etc.

And thus it goes on for pages ; but in spite of the absurd form the idea appears clearly. Nothing but spontaneousness is worth anything ; and the form itself is contempt for all that is orderly, correct, and systematic. The manners also which shocked not a little the pedantic and economical inhabitants of the Alps corresponded to these forms of style, when the young enthusiasts of

the North came as on a pilgrimage to the Zürich
apostle, foremost among them the two Stolbergs,
displaying their long fair locks in the midst of
those carefully powdered heads, and dividing 'the
green waves of the lake' in full daylight. Who
does not think of old Horace?

Ingenium misera quia fortunatius arte
Credit et excludit sanos Helicone poetas
Democritus, bona pars non ungues ponere curat, etc.

Still the true field of battle, that of literary
principles, which at that time had alone the power
of exciting a passionate interest in Germany, after Frederick's heroic period had
Strassburg.
been succeeded by his more prosaic administrative
activity, the true battle-field was the valley of the
Rhine, where historical ideas and interests at all
times were wont to meet and join in conflict. It was
in Strassburg that Goethe met with unfortunate
Lenz, the most gifted perhaps of his friends, a
morbid and misunderstood genius, who, like many
of his generation, was to sink, while still young,
into the night of insanity; with honest Lerse,
whom he immortalised in his 'Götz;' with that
strange and kind-hearted dreamer, Jung-Stilling,
the tailor-doctor, a sweet and touching physiog-
nomy, an ardent and mystical soul, whom Goethe

revealed to the world by publishing the manuscript
of his diary ; with Herder above all, who was then
suffering from an operation on his eyes, and with
whom he kept company in the long winter evenings
of 1770–71. Here took place those conversations,
and that interchange of thought, awakened by their
reading which made that year a memorable date,
and the city of Strassburg, still entirely German
in spite of ninety years of French government, a
hallowed spot to the German people. Here it was
that young Goethe—then twenty-one years old—
who had recently arrived from Leipzig with somewhat academical or rather arcadian views and
habits of mind, was initiated into the beauties of
Shakespeare by Herder. Here it was that they
read and re-read the ' Vicar of Wakefield,' 'Tristram
Shandy,' Percy's ' Reliques,' and of course Ossian ;
and here, also, that Goethe, while under the
charm of the most poetical romance of his life,
composed his finest lyric poems, sketched his
' Götz,' and conceived the idea of ' Faust.' The
account he has left in his memoirs of the time he
spent in Alsace, the portraits he has traced of the
companions of his generous freaks there, the description we owe to him of the movement of ideas
which animated this sparkling, stirring young

generation, is simply a masterpiece of literary history in the modest frame of a personal memoir.

From Strassburg Goethe returned to his native town, Frankfurt, where he at first settled under the paternal roof—the *casa santa*, as the poet's friends used to call it—and afterwards took up his residence at Wetzlar as a clerk to the Imperial Court of Justice. There, assisted by his friend Merck—a shrewd and deep mind of severe literary taste, with whom he was always to be seen, ' like Faust and Mephistopheles '—he edited the chief paper of the party, the ' Frankfurter Gelehrte Anzeigen,' and published stroke upon stroke ' Götz,' ' Werther,' ' Clavigo.' Here ' Socrates-Addison,' as they called Merck, replaced the ' Irish dean with his whip '—so they styled Herder—in the tutorship of Goethe, the ' young lord with scraping cock-spurs.' Literary congresses were soon organised everywhere in the valleys of the Lahn, Mein, and Rhine. Jacobi, the philosopher of sentiment, opened his hospitable villa of Pempelfort to his numerous friends; Sophie de la Roche—the authoress of ' Fräulein von Sternheim,' the first love of Wieland's youth, the mother of Maximiliane Brentano, who furnished more than one feature to Goethe's ' Lotte,' the

Frankfurt.

grandmother of Clemens Brentano, the romanticist, and Bettina, 'the child'—Sophie de la
Roche received them often in her seat near Co-
blentz. The little University of Giessen, where
proud Klinger, the dramatist, who has given the
name to the whole period, was then studying, and
already shaping out that wonderful career which
he began as a poor workman's apprentice and
ended as a Russian lieutenant-general; the old
imperial city of Wetzlar, where the scene of
Goethe's 'Werther' is laid, as it was the real
scene of the poet's and Lotte's love; the small
residence of Darmstadt, where Merck received the
visits of all the literary celebrities of the day—saw
in turn the meetings where the new creed was
enthusiastically preached.

It was under Merck's guidance that Goethe,
together with his brother-in-law, Schlosser, and
Herder, set to work so vigorously and mercilessly
to attack the old literary routine in his periodical,
upon which Göze, Lessing's old theological enemy,
invoked the rigour of the secular arm ; and when we
see Merck ' knock the powder out of the wigs ' in
his young friend's journal, it is not difficult to
understand how Wieland could say of him :
' Merck is among critics what Klopstock is among

poets, Herder among the learned, Lavater among
Christians, and Goethe among all human beings.'
But with all his impatience for conventional
literature, and in spite of his appreciation of that
simple, unaffected popular poetry which Herder
had brought into fashion, Merck never suffered
himself to be deceived by counterfeit nature *à la*
Macpherson. True, he ridiculed the tight-laced
poetry of the times, and had no mercy for classical
buskin; but he was quite as severe upon the two
impetuous Stolbergs' strained enthusiasm, upon
whimsical Lenz's intentional eccentricity, and
tender-hearted Jacobi's mystic languor. In the
midst of all these young folks giving themselves
the airs of tribunes or seers—more than one of
them had indeed a deceptive likeness to genius—he
did not hesitate a moment in distinguishing the
only real genius, Wolfgang Apollo. It was Merck
also who made him known to the young Duke of
Saxe-Weimar, henceforth his protector and friend
for life.

Goethe was twenty-six years old when he accepted (1775) the invitation of Charles
Augustus, and transported to Weimar the
tone and the *allures* of the literary Bohemia of
Strassburg. There, to the terror of the good

Weimar.

M

burghers of that small residence, to the still
greater terror of the microscopic courtiers, began
that 'genial' and wild life, which he and his
august companion led during several years.
Hunting, riding on horseback, masquerades,
private theatricals, satirical verse, improvisation
of all sorts, flirtation particularly, filled up day
and night, to the scandal of all worthy folks, who
were utterly at a loss to account for His Serene
Highness saying '*Du*' to this Frankfurt *roturier*.
The gay Dowager Duchess, Wieland's firm friend,
looked upon these juvenile freaks with a more
lenient eye ; for she well knew that the fermen-
tation once over, a noble, generous wine would
remain.   'We are playing the devil here,' writes
Goethe to Merck ; 'we hold together, the Duke
and I, and go our own way.   Of course, in doing
so we knock against the wicked, and also against
the good ; but we shall succeed ; for the gods are
evidently on our side.'   Soon Herder was to join
them there, unfortunately not always satisfied
with the results of his teaching about absolute
liberty of genius.

The whole generation bore with impatience,
as we have seen, the yoke of the established
order, of authority under whatever form, whether

the fetters were those of literary convention or
social prejudice, of the State or the Church. The
ego affirmed its absolute, inalienable right; The general attitude
of the ge-
neration. it strove to manifest itself according to
its caprices, and refused to acknow-
ledge any check. Individual inspiration was a
sacred thing, which reality with its rules and
prejudices could only spoil and deflower. Now,
according to the temperament of each, they rose
violently against society and its laws, or resigned
themselves silently to a dire necessity. The one
in Titanic effort climbed Olympus, heaving Pelion
on Ossa; the other wiped a furtive tear out of his
eye, and, aspiring to deliverance, dreamed of an
ideal happiness. Sometimes in the same poet the
two dispositions succeed each other.

Cover thy sky with vapour and clouds, O Zeus, exclaims Goethe's Prometheus, and practise thy strength on
tops of oaks and summits of mountains like the child who
beheads thistles. Thou must, nevertheless, leave me my
earth and my hut, which thou hast not built, and my
hearth, whose flame thou enviest. Is it not my heart,
burning with a sacred ardour, which alone has accomplished all? And should I thank thee, who wast sleeping
whilst I worked?

The same young man, who had put in o the mouth

M 2

of the rebellious Titan this haughty and defiant
outburst, at other moments, when he was dis-
couraged and weary of the struggle, took refuge
within himself.   Like *Werther*, 'finding his world
within himself, he spoils and caresses his tender
heart, like a sickly child, all whose caprices we in-
dulge.'   One or the other of those attitudes towards
reality, the active and the passive, were soon taken
by the whole youth of the time; and just as
Schiller's ' Brigands ' gave birth to a whole series
of wild dramas, 'Werther' left in the novels of the
time a long line of tears.   More than that, even in
reality *Karl Moor* found imitators who engaged in
an open struggle against society, and one met
at every corner languishing *Siegwarts*, whose
delicate soul was hurt by the cruel contact of the
world.

What strikes us most in this morbid sentimentality, is the eternal melancholy sighing
after nature.   Ossian's cloudy sadness and
Young's dark Nights veil every brow.   They fly
into the solitudes of the forests in order to dream
freely of a less brutal world.   They must, indeed,
have been very far from nature to seek for it with
such·avidity.   Many, in fact, of these ardent,
feverish young men became in the end a prey,

some to madness, others to suicide. A species of
moral epidemic, like that which followed upon
the apparent failure of the Revolution in 1799,
had broken out. The germ of Byronism may be
clearly detected already in the Wertherism of
those times. Exaggerated and overstrained
imaginations found insufficient breathing-room in
the world, and met on all sides with boundaries
to their unlimited demands. Hearts, accustomed
to follow the dictates of their own inspiration
alone, bruised themselves against the sharp angles
of reality. The thirst for action which consumed
their ardent youth could not be quenched, in fact,
in the narrow limits of domestic life; and public
life did not exist. Frederick had done great
things, but only, like the three hundred other
German governments, to exclude the youth of
the middle classes from active life. Thence the
general uneasiness. 'Werther' was as much an
effect as a cause of this endemic disease; above
all, it was the expression of a general state of
mind. It is this which constitutes its historical
importance, while the secret of its lasting value
is to be found in its artistic form.

Besides, if I may say so without paradox, the
disease was but an excess of health, a juvenile

crisis through which Herder, young Goethe, Schiller, and indeed the whole generation, had to pass.

Oh (exclaimed old Goethe fifty years later in a conversation with young Felix Mendelssohn)—oh, if I could but write a fourth volume of my life. . . . It should be a history of the year 1775, which no one knows or can write better than I. How the nobility, feeling itself outrun by the middle classes, began to do all it could not to be left behind in the race; how liberalism, jacobinism, and all that devilry awoke : how a new life began · how we studied, and poetised, made love and wasted our time; how we young folks, full of life and activity, but awkward as we could be, scoffed at the aristocratic propensities of Messrs. Nicolaï and Co. in Berlin, who at that time reigned supreme. . . . Ah, yes, that was a spring, when everything was budding and shooting, when more than one tree was yet bare, while others were already full of leaves. All that in the year 1775 !

Old pedantic Nicolaï, at whom he scoffed thus, foresaw, with his prosy common- sense, what would happen 'with all those confounded striplings,' as Wieland called them, 'who gave themselves airs as if they were accustomed to play at blind-man's buff with Shakespeare.' 'In four or five years,' said he in 1776, 'this fine enthusiasm will have passed away like smoke; a few drops of spirit will be found in the empty helmet, and a big *caput mortuum* in the crucible.' This proved true certainly for the great majority, but not so as regards the two coursers which then broke loose, and for him who had cut their traces and released them. Of the latter I have spoken to-day; of the former two I shall say something the next time we meet. Not of their youth, however, but of their maturer age; not of their views when they were twenty, but of the philosophy which they had come to twenty years later. Goethe, indeed, modified, or at least cleared up, his early views under the influence of a deeper study of nature and the sight of ancient and Renaissance Art in Italy (1786-1788); Schiller put himself to school under Kant (1790), and went out of it with a completely altered philosophy; Kant himself became another after, if not in consequence of, the great King's death (1786); Herder alone remained faithful throughout to the creed he had himself preached.

I have dwelt so long on Herder not only because, till lately, his influence has not been sufficiently acknowledged, but also because the way opened by him, although partly and temporarily abandoned during the classical period of which I shall have to speak to you the next time, was followed again by the third generation

Conclusion.

of the founders of German culture, the so-called
Romanticists, and by all the great scholars, who,
in the first half of this century, revived the historical sciences in Germany. Herder's ideas have,
indeed, penetrated our whole thought to such a
degree, whilst his works are so unfinished and
disconnected, that it is hardly possible for us to
account for the extraordinary effect these ideas and
works produced in their day, except by marking the
contrast which they present with the then reigning
methods and habits, as well as the surprising influence exercised by Herder personally. From his
twenty-fifth year, indeed, he was a sovereign.
His actual and uncontested sway was not, it is
true, prolonged beyond a period of about sixteen
years, albeit his name figured to a much later time
on the list of living potentates. It is also true, that
when the seeds thrown by him had grown luxuri-
antly, and were bearing fruit, the sower was almost
entirely forgotten or wilfully ignored. The generation, however, of the ' Stürmer und Dränger,' or,
as they were pleased to denominate themselves,
the ' original geniuses,' looked up to Herder as
their leader and prophet. Some of them turned
from him later on and went back to the exclusive
worship of classical antiquity ; but their very

manner of doing homage to it bore witness to
Herder's influence. The following generation
threw itself no less exclusively into the middle
ages; but what, after all, was it doing if not following Herder's example, when it raked up Dantes
and Calderons out of the dust in order to confront
them with and oppose them to Virgils and Racines?
However they might repudiate, nay even forget,
their teacher, his doctrines already pervaded the
whole intellectual atmosphere of Germany, and
men's minds breathed them in with the very air
they inhaled. To-day they belong to Europe.

Herder, I repeat, is certainly neither a classical
nor a finished writer. He has no doubt gone
out of fashion, because his style is pompous and
diffuse, his composition loose or fragmentary;
because his reasoning lacks firmness and his erudition solidity. Still, no other German writer of note
exercised the important indirect influence which
was exercised by Herder. In this I do not allude
to Schelling and his philosophy, which received
more than one impulse from Herder's ideas; nor
to Hegel, who reduced them to a metaphysical
system and defended them with his wonderful
dialectics. But F. A. Wolf, when he points out to
us in Homer·the process of epic poetry; Niebuhr,

in revealing to us the growth of Rome, the birth
of her religious and national legends, the slow,
gradual formation of her marvellous constitution;
Savigny, when he proves that the Roman Civil
Law, that masterpiece of human ingenuity, was
not the work of a wise legislator, but rather the
wisdom of generations and of centuries; Eichhorn,
when he wrote the history of German law and
created thereby a new branch of historical science
which has proved one of the most fertile; A.
W. Schlegel and his school, when they trans-
planted all the poetry of other nations to Germany
by means of imitations which are real wonders
of assimilation; Frederick Schlegel, when, in the
' Wisdom of the Hindoos,' he opened out that
vast field of comparative linguistic science, which
Bopp and so many others have since cultivated
with such success; Alexander von Humboldt and
Karl Ritter, when they gave a new life to geo-
graphy by showing the earth in its growth and
development and coherence; W. von Humboldt,
when he established the laws of language as well as
those of self-government; Jacob Grimm, when he
brought German philology into existence, while his
brother Wilhelm made a science of Northern mythology; still later on, D. F. Strauss, when, in the days

of our own youth, he placed the myth and the legend, with their unconscious origin and growth, not alone in opposition to the idea of Deity intervening to interrupt established order, but also to that of imposture and conscious fraud; Otfr. Müller, when he proved that Greek mythology, far from containing moral abstractions or historical facts, is the involuntary personification of surrounding nature, subsequently developed by imagination; Max Müller even, when he creates the new science of comparative mythology—what else are they doing but applying and working out Herder's ideas? And if we turn our eyes to other nations, what else were Burke and Coleridge, B. Constant and A. Thierry, Guizot and A. de Tocqueville—what are Renan and Taine, Carlyle and Darwin doing, each in his own branch, but applying and developing Herder's two fundamental principles, that of organic evolution and that of the entireness of the individual? For it was Herder who discovered the true spirit of history, and in this sense it is that Goethe was justified in saying of him:

A noble mind, desirous of fathoming man's soul in whatever direction it may shoot forth, searcheth throughout the universe for sound and word which flow through the lands in a thousand sources and brooks; wanders

through the oldest as the newest regions and listens in
every zone. . . . He knew how to find this soul wherever it lay hid, whether robed in grave disguise, or lightly
clothed in the garb of play, in order to found for the
future this lofty rule : Humanity be our eternal aim !

LECTURE V.

AMONG the young literary rebels who, under
Herder's guidance, attempted, towards and after
1775, to overthrow all conventionalism, all authority, even all law and rule, in order to put in their
stead the absolute self-government of genius,
freed from all tutorship—the foremost were the
two greatest German poets, Goethe and Schiller.
Goethe's 'Götz' and 'Werther,' Schiller's 'Brigands,' and 'Cabal and Love,' were greeted as the
promising forerunners of the national literature to
come. Their subjects were German and modern,
not French or classic; in their plan they affected
Shakespearean liberty; in their language they
were at once familiar, strong, and original; in

their inspiration they were protests against the social prejudices and political abuses of the time, vehement outbursts of individuality against convention.

Not twenty years had passed away, when both the revolutionists had become calm and resigned liberal conservatives, who understood and taught that liberty is possible only under the empire of law; that the real world with all its limits had a right as well as the inner world, which knows no frontiers; that to be completely free man must fly into the ideal sphere of Art, Science, or formless Religion. Not that they abjured 'the dreams of their youth.' The nucleus of their new creed was contained in their first belief; but it had been developed into a system of social views more in harmony with society and its exigencies, of æsthetic opinions more independent of reality and its accidents, of philosophical ideas more speculative and methodical. In other words, Goethe and Schiller never ceased to believe as they had done at twenty, that all vital creations in nature as in society are the result of growth and organic development, not of intentional, self-conscious planning, and that individuals on their part act powerfully only through their nature in its entirety, not through one faculty alone, such as reason or will, separated from instinct, imagination, temperament, passion, etc. Only they came to the conviction that there existed general laws which presided over organic development, and that there was a means of furthering in the individual the harmony between temperament, character, understanding, and imagination, without sacrificing one to the others. Hence they shaped for themselves a general view of Nature and Mankind, Society and History, which may not have become the permanent view of the whole nation; but which for a time was predominant, which even now is still held by many, and which in some respects will always be the ideal of the best men in Germany, even when circumstances have wrought a change in the intellectual and social conditions of their country, so as to necessitate a total transformation and accommodation of those views.

We cannot regard it merely as the natural effect of advancing years, if Goethe and Schiller modified and cleared their views; if Kant, whose great emancipating act, the 'Critic of Pure Reason,' falls chronologically in the preceding period (1781), corrected what seemed to him too absolute in his

system, and reconstructed from the basis of the
conscience that metaphysical world which he had
destroyed by his analysis of the intellect. The
world just then was undergoing profound changes.
The great 'Philosopher King' had descended to
the tomb (1786), and with him the absolute
liberty of thought, which had reigned for forty-
six years. The French Revolution, after having
exalted all generous souls, and seemingly confirmed the triumph of liberty and justice which
the generation had witnessed in America, took a
direction and drifted into excesses which unde-
ceived, sobered, and saddened even the most
hopeful believers. As regards personal circumstances, the Italian journey of Goethe (1786–1788)
and his scientific investigations into nature, the
study of Kant's new philosophy to which Schiller
submitted his undisciplined mind (1790 and 1791),
were the high-schools out of which their genius
came strengthened and purified, although their
æsthetic and moral doctrines did not remain quite
unimpaired by them.   I shall endeavour to give an
idea of this double process and its results at the risk
of being still more abstract and dry than before.[1]

[1] For the following pages on Goethe, see his 'Wilhelm
Meister,' especially the sixth book, and 'Bildung und Umbildung

Man is the last and highest link in Nature; his task is to understand what she aims at in him and then to fulfil her intentions. This view of Herder's was Goethe's starting-point in the formation of his *Weltanschauung* or general view of things.

All the world (says one of the characters in 'Wilhelm Meister') lies before us, like a vast quarry before the architect. He does not deserve the name, if he does not compose with these accidental natural materials an image whose source is in his mind, and if he does not do it with the greatest possible economy, solidity, and perfection. All that we find outside of us, nay, within us, is object-matter; but deep within us lives also a power capable of giving an ideal form to this matter. This creative power allows us no rest till we have produced that ideal form in one or the other way, either without us in finished works, or in our own life.

Here we already have in germ Schiller's idea that life ought to be a work of art. But how do we achieve this task, continually impeded as we are by circumstances and by our fellow-creatures, who will not always leave us in peace to develop our individual characters in perfect conformity with

organischer Naturen,' particularly 'Geschichte meines Botanischen Studiums' (vol. xxxvi. of the 'Works').

nature? In our relations with our neighbour,
Goethe (like Lessing and Wieland, Kant and
Herder, and all the great men of his and the preceding age, in England and France as well as in
Germany) recommended absolute toleration not
only of opinions, but also of individualities, particularly those in which Nature manifests herself
'undefiled.' As to circumstances, which is only
another name for Fate, he preached and practised
resignation. At every turn of our life, in fact,
we meet with limits; our intelligence has its
frontiers which bar its way; our senses are limited,
and can only embrace an infinitely small part of
nature; few of our wishes can be fulfilled; privation and sufferings await us at every moment.
'Privation is thy lot, privation! That is the
eternal song which resounds at every moment,
which, our whole life through, each hour sings
hoarsely to our ears!' laments Faust. What
remains then for man? 'Everything cries to us
that we must *resign* ourselves.' 'There are few
men, however, who, conscious of the privations
and sufferings in store for them in life, and desirous
to avoid the necessity of resigning themselves
anew in each particular case, have the courage to
perform the act of resignation once for all;' who

say to themselves that there are eternal and necessary laws to which we must submit, and that we
had better do it without grumbling; who 'endeavour to form principles which are not liable to
be destroyed, but are rather confirmed by contact
with reality.' In other words, when man has
discovered the laws of nature, both moral and
physical, he must accept them as the limits of his
actions and desires; he must not wish for eternity
of life or inexhaustible capacities of enjoyment,
understanding, and acting, any more than he
wishes for the moon. For rebellion against these
laws must needs be an act of impotency as well as
of deceptive folly. By resignation, on the contrary,
serene resignation, the human soul is purified;
for thereby it becomes free of selfish passions and
arrives at that intellectual superiority in which
the contemplation and understanding of things
give sufficient contentment, without making it
needful for man to stretch out his hands to take
possession of them: a thought which Goethe's
friend, Schiller, has magnificently developed in
his grand philosophical poems. Optimism and
pessimism disappear at once as well as fatalism;
the highest and most refined intellect again accepts
the world, as children and ignorant toilers do, as

a given necessity. He does not even think the world could be otherwise, and within its limits he not only enjoys and suffers, but also works gaily, trying, like Horace, to subject things to himself, but resigned to submit to them, when they are invincible. Thus the simple Hellenic existence which, contrary to Christianity, but according to nature, accepted the present without ceaselessly thinking of death and another world, and acted in that present and in the circumstances allotted to each by fate, without wanting to overstep the boundaries of nature, would revive again in our modern world and free us for ever from the torment of unaccomplished wishes and of vain terrors.

The sojourn in Italy, during which Goethe lived outside the struggle for life, outside the competition and contact of practical activity, in the contemplation of nature and art, developed this view—the spectator's view, which will always be that of the artist and of the thinker, strongly opposed to that of the actor on the stage of human life. ‘Iphigenia,’ ‘Torquato Tasso,’ ‘Wilhelm Meister’ are the fruits and the interpreters of this conception of the moral world. What ripened and perfected it, so as to raise it into a general view, not only of

Goethe's view of Nature.

morality, but also of the great philosophical questions which man is called upon to answer, was his study of nature, greatly furthered during his stay in Italy. The problem which lay at the bottom of all the vague longing of his generation for nature *he* was to solve. It became his incessant endeavour to understand the coherence and unity of nature.

You are for ever searching for what is necessary in nature (Schiller wrote to him once), but you search for it by the most difficult way. You take the whole of nature in order to obtain light on the particular case; you look into the totality for the explanation of the individual existence. From the simplest organism (in nature), you ascend step by step to the more complicated, and finally construct the most complicated of all, man, out of the materials of the whole of nature. In thus creating man anew under the guidance of nature, you penetrate into his mysterious organism.

And, indeed, as there is a wonderful harmony with nature in Goethe, the poet and the man, so there is the same harmony in Goethe, the savant and the thinker; nay, even science he practised as a poet. As one of the greatest physicists of our days, Helmholtz, has said of him: ' He did not try to translate nature into abstract conceptions, but takes it as a complete work of art, which

must reveal its contents spontaneously to an
intelligent observer.' Goethe never became a
thorough experimentalist; he did not want ' to
extort the secret from nature by pumps and re-
torts.' He waited patiently for a voluntary revelation, *i.e.* until he could surprise that secret by an
intuitive glance; for it was his conviction that
if you live intimately with Nature, she will sooner
or later disclose her mysteries to you. If you read
his ' Songs,' his ' Werther,' his ' Wahlverwandt-
schaften,' you feel that extraordinary intimacy—
I had almost said identification—with nature, present everywhere. Werther's love springs up with
the blossom of all nature; he begins to sink and
nears his self-made tomb, while autumn, the death
of nature, is in the fields and woods. So does
the moon spread her mellow light over his garden,
as ' the mild eye of a true friend over his destiny.'
Never was there a poet who humanised nature or
naturalised human feeling, if I might say so, to
the same degree as Goethe. Now, this same love
of nature he brought into his scientific researches.

He began his studies of nature early, and he
began them as he was to finish them, with geology.
Buffon's great views on the revolutions of the earth
had made a deep impression upon him, although

he was to end as the declared adversary of that
vulcanism which we can trace already at the
bottom of Buffon's theory—naturally enough, when
we think how uncongenial all violence in society
and nature was to him, how he looked everywhere
for slow, uninterrupted evolution. From theoretical study he had early turned to direct observation ; and when his administrative functions
obliged him to survey the mines of the little
Dukedom, ample opportunity was offered for
positive studies. As early as 1778, in a paper on
Granite, he wrote : ' I do not fear the reproach
that a spirit of contradiction draws me from the
contemplation of the human heart—this most
mobile, most mutable and fickle part of the creation
—to the observation of (granite) the oldest, firmest,
deepest, most immovable son of Nature. For all
natural things are in connexion with each other.'
It was his life's task to search for the links of this
coherence in order to find that unity, which he
knew to be in the moral as well as material universe.

From those ' first and most solid beginnings of
our existence,' he turned to the history of plants
and to the anatomy of the animals which cover
this crust of the earth. The study of Spinoza,

confirmed him in the direction thus taken. 'There
I am on and under the mountains, seeking the
divine *in herbis et lapidibus*,' says he, in Spinoza's
own words; and again : 'Pardon me, if I like to
remain silent, when people speak of a divine being
which I can know only in *rebus singularibus*.' This
pantheistic view grew stronger and stronger with
years; but it became a pantheism very different
from that of Parmenides, for whom being and
thinking are one, or from that of Giordano Bruno,
which rests on the analogy of a universal soul
with the human soul, or even from that of Spinoza
himself, which takes its start from the relations of
the physical world with the conceptive world, and
of both with the divine one.   Goethe's pantheism
always tends to dis·over the cohesion of the
members of nature, of which man is one : if once
he has discovered this universal unity, where there
are no gaps in space, nor leaps in time, he need
not search further for the divine.

Nature !   We live in it and remain strangers to it.
It continually talks to us and does not betray its secret.
It seems to have planned everything with a view to indi-
viduality, and does not care for individuals.   It lives only
by continual birth, and the mother is indiscernible.
Nature has thought, and does not cease to think; but it

thinks, not as man does, but as Nature. It loves itself
and is ever centred on itself with innumerable eyes and
hearts. It has multiplied itself in order to enjoy itself
a hundredfold. It is ever creating new enjoyers, never
tired of communicating itself. Life is its most beautiful
invention, and death its artifice for having much life.

This idea it was which was afterwards meta-
physically developed by Schelling and Hegel ; but
metaphysics are not what we are now studying.
Even when I shall have to speak by and by of
Kant, who entirely changed the basis of all speculative thought, I shall leave aside his philosophy
proper as much as possible, and try only to speak
of his way of looking at life and history. Goethe's
view of life, which he won through the study of
nature, and which consists in trying to seize the
unity of nature in the constant climax of its
phenomena up to the highest, the intellectual
phenomenon, man,—differs from all former similar
views in this, that it considers the coherence of the
universe as a *process* in time, a history in which
or through which nature becomes conscious of
itself, not as a connection by links in space only.
This is the point where Herder's influence is most
perceptible, and which was to be brought into a
system by the methodical and dialectical specula-

tions of Hegel, whom we may consider as the great
summariser of all the intellectual work done by
Germany during the sixty or seventy years with
which we are occupied.

By what means was this process, this history,
which Goethe discerned in the coherence of nature,
to be discovered and understood? By the means
of the very same organ of *intuition* which the
whole generation of Herder and Goethe had recognised in their youth as the highest of poetical
faculties, and which Kant himself had admitted
to be the distinctive quality of the poet. Others,
we have seen and shall further see, applied this
faculty to history. Goethe applied it to nature.
His poet's eye revealed to him the mystery of
nature's laws; but he was not content with such
divination. He became a patient and conscien-
tious observer, and did not rest until he had, as it
were, proved his sum. Now, this method has remained the dominant one in Germany, and has
misled thinkers more than once, when they applied
it without controlling it by the inductive method.
The aberrations and excrescences of Schelling's
philosophy of Nature are in everybody's memory;
and the best things done in natural science, even
in Germany, have been done by adversaries of

Schelling's school and adherents of the mechanical
principle of explanation. Nevertheless the intuitive method has been wcrderfully fertile even
for natural science, and I remember how often
Liebig himself told me that all his discoveries had
been the result of lightning-like intuition and
divination, ascertained afterwards by observation
and experiment. As for historical sciences, the
conquests made by the intuitive method are
uncontested. It has taught the world that the
knowledge of laws—that is to say, the most abstract and unreal kind of knowledge—is by no
means alone valuable; that causality, to which
the savants of our day would again limit all
science, is not its sole object; that the intuitive
knowledge of typical forms—in other words, of
platonic ideas—which we acquire by the careful
observation of individual and particular phenomena,
has equally its value; for it allows us to form ideas
of things, which always remain the same through
all the changes of the phenomena, and nevertheless do not exist in reality.

It is analogy which helps us to form these
intuitive or platonic ideas. It was through
analogy that Goethe arrived at his great discoveries in natural science, and I only repeat

what such men as Johannes Müller, Baer, and
Helmholtz have been willing to acknowledge,
when I say that the poet's eye has been as keen as
that of any naturalist.   Kant had contended that
there might be a superior Intelligence, which,
contrary to human intelligence, goes from the
general to the particular; and Goethe thought—
he proved, I might say—that in man too some of
this divine intelligence can operate and shine, if
only in isolated sparks.   It was a spark of this
kind which, first at Padua on the sight of a fan-
palm tree, then again, on the eve of his departure
from Palermo, during a walk in the public garden
amidst the southern vegetation, revealed to him
the law of the metamorphosis of plants.   He found
an analogy between the different parts of the same
plant which seemed to repeat themselves : unity
and evolution were revealed to him at once.

Three years later the sight of a half-broken
sheep-skull, which he found by chance on the
sand of the Venetian Lido, taught him that the
same law, as he had suspected, applied also to
vertebrate animals, and that the skull might be
considered as a series of strongly modified ver-
tebræ.   He had, in fact, already hinted at the
principle, shortly after put forward by Lamarck,

and long afterwards developed and firmly established
by Darwin. He considered the difference in the
anatomical structure of animal species as modifications of a type or planned structure, modifications brought about by the difference of life,
food, and dwellings. He had discovered as early
as 1786 the intermaxillary bone in man, *i.e.* the
remnant of a part which had had to be adapted
to the exigencies of the changed structure; and
proved thereby that there had been a primitive
similarity of structure, which had been trans-
formed by development of some parts, and
atrophy of others. Goethe's sketch of an 'Introduction into Comparative Anatomy,' which
he wrote in 1795, urged by A. von Humboldt,
has remained, if I may believe those competent to
judge, a fundamental stone of modern science.
And, I may be allowed, as I am unversed in such
matters, to invoke the authority of one of the most
eminent living physiologists, Helmholtz, who says
of Goethe's anatomical essay, that in it the poet

. . . . teaches, with the greatest clearness and decision,
that all differences in the structure of animal species are to
be considered as changes of one fundamental type, which
have been brought about by fusion, transformation, ag-
grandisement, diminution, or total annihilation of several

parts. This has, indeed, become, in the present state of
comparative anatomy, the leading idea of this science. It
has never since been expressed better or more clearly than
by Goethe : and after-times have made few essential
modifications.[1]

Now, the same may be said, I am told, in spite
of some differences as to details, of his metamorphosis of plants. I do not mean by this to say
that Goethe is the real author of the theory of
evolution. There is between him and Mr. Darwin
the difference which there is between Vico and
Niebuhr, Herder and F. A. Wolf. In the one case
we have a fertile hint, in the other a well-
established system, worked out by proofs and
convincing arguments. Nevertheless, when a
man like Johannes Müller sees in Goethe's views
' the presentiment of a distant ideal of natural
history,' we may be allowed to see in Goethe one
of the fathers of the doctrine of evolution, which,
after all, is only an application of Herder's principle of *fieri* to the material world.

After having thus gone through the whole
series of organisms, from the simplest to the most
complicated, Goethe finds that he has laid, as it
were, the last crowning stone of the universal

[1] Written in 1853, five years before the appearance of Mr.
Darwin's great work.

pyramid, raised from the materials of the whole quarry of nature ; that he has reconstructed man. And here begins a new domain ; for after all for mankind the *highest* study must be man himself.   The social problems of property, education, marriage, occupied Goethe's mind all his life through, although more particularly in the last thirty years.   The relations of man with nature, the question how far he is free from the laws of necessity, how far subject to them, are always haunting him.   If you read the 'Wahl-verwandtschaften,' the 'Wanderjahre,' the second 'Faust,' you will find those grave questions approached from all sides.   I shall not, however, enter here into an exposition of Goethe's political, social, and educational views, not only because they mostly belong to a later period, but especially because they have never found a wide echo, nor determined the opinions of an important portion of the nation, nor entered as integrating principles into its lay creed.   Not so with the metaphysical conclusion which he reached by this path, and which is somewhat different from the pantheism of his youth, inasmuch as he combines with it somewhat of the fundamental ideas of Leibnitz, which were also Lessing's, and which, after all, form a

Goethe's philosophic views.

sort of return to Christianity, as understood in its
widest sense, in the sense in which it harmonises
with Plato's idealism. 'Thinking is not to be
severed from what is thought, nor will from movement.' Nature consequently is God, and God is
nature, but in this God-Nature man lives as an
imperishable monad, capable of going through
thousands of metamorphoses, but destined to rest
on each stage of this unlimited existence, in full
possession of the present, in which he has to expand his whole being by action or enjoyment.
This conception of life was not, as you will see,
the creation of an imagination longing to pass
beyond the conditions of human existence—which
is the idealism of the 'general'— but the highest
result of the poet's insight into the order of nature.

Here we mark the great contrast with the
later Kant, the contrast between a view which
sees in man one link in the chain of nature, and
the view which takes man out of the order of
nature and makes him a member of a higher
invisible order. This contrast has filled up the
intellectual history of Germany ever since Herder
opened hostilities against the master of his youth.
In vain Fichte, Schelling, Hegel gave themselves
out to be the disciples of Kant; in reality they

were only the sophists, who, with the weapons of
Kant's dialecticism, carried *ad absurdum* the main
idea of Herder and Goethe, the German idea, κατ'
ἐξοχήν, according to which nature is immanent in
the human mind, and develops itself by the developing of the conceptions of this mind. For
mind is nothing else but nature come to the consciousness of itself: its essence being the essence
of nature, its contents the contents of nature.
The task of the student is to discover this identity,
and the most powerful vehicle for its discovery is
intuition. Now, as long as in these matters intuition let itself be controlled by observation and
induction, it had wonderful results, particularly
in the historical sciences and even in the natural
sciences, although, as I just said, the best part of
Germany's work in the latter was done by adversaries of this method. Still, A. von Humboldt,
when he declared his aim to be 'the consideration
of physical things as a whole, moved and animated
by inner forces,' and K. Ritter, when he defined
'the earth as a cosmic individual with a particular
organisation, an *ens sui generis*, with progressive
development,' both stood on common ground with
Goethe and Herder; on common ground even
with Schelling, whose influence has been so de-

O

plorable on natural science in Germany, leading to
the most dangerous consequences through the
desire to understand and grasp the parts, their
distribution and ordination, by starting from the
whole—a sort of deductive system of intuition as
the old deductive system was one of abstract
conceptions. What, on the contrary, the intuitive method, supported by severe and sagacious
criticism of detail, has produced in the historical
sciences, which can only be grasped by intuition,
I need not say. The names of F. A. Wolf and
Niebuhr, W. von Humboldt and Bopp, the Grimms
and Boeckh, Savigny and Eichhorn, tell us clearly
enough. Philology and archæology, theology and
mythology, jurisprudence and history proper, have
been entirely renewed by it; whilst linguistic
and literary history may be said to have been
created by it. (I am here only explaining the
views of the creators of German culture: 1 do
not defend them, where I share them, as I did
not criticise them when I found myself at variance
with them. Else, I should certainly pause here,
and in all courtesy break a lance with those men
of the younger generation and of this island, who
would treat the historical sciences by the same
method as the natural or mathematical.)

I have said that there was an antagonism between Kant's views and those of Herder and Goethe, and that this antagonism has The Two Currents. been ever since sensibly felt in the intel- lectual history of Germany. Some efforts were made to reconcile them, as for instance by Schiller. Sometimes a sort of alliance took place, as in 1813, when the romanticists, who were quite under the spell of the Herder-Goethe ideas, invoked the aid of the moral energy, which was a special characteristic of Kant's disciples ; but the antagonism lives on not the less even now in the German nation, as the antagonism between Hume and Burke, Locke and Berkeley, Fielding and Richardson, Shakespeare and Milton, nay, between Renaissance and Puritan- ism in spite of their apparent death, is still living in the English nation. This difference is, as will happen in this world, much more the difference between two dispositions of mind, character, and temperament, than between two opposite theories ; or at least the conflicting opinions are much more the result of our moral and intellectual dispositions than of objective observation and abstract argu- mentation. Germany owes much to the stern unflinching moral principles of Kant; she owes still more, however, to the serene and large views

of Goethe. The misfortune of both ideals is that
they cannot and will never be accessible save to
a small *élite*, that of Kant to a moral, that of
Goethe to an intellectual *élite*. But are not all
ideals of an essentially aristocratic nature ? The
German ideals, however, are so more than others,
and the consequence has been a wide gap between
the mass of the nation and the minority which has
been true to those ideals. The numerical majority,
indeed, of the German nation has either remained
faithful to the Church, though without fanaticism, or has become materialistic and rationalistic.
It is a great misfortune for a nation when its
greatest writer in his greatest works is only
understood by the happy few, and when its
greatest moralist preaches a moral which is above
the common force of human nature. The only
means of union between the nation and the intellectual and moral aristocracy, which has kept
and guarded that treasure, as well as the only
link between these two aristocratic views of life
themselves, would be furnished by religion, a
religion such as Lessing, Mendelssohn, and above
all Schleiermacher, propounded, such as reigned
all over Germany forty or fifty years ago, before
party spirit had set to work, and the flattest of

rationalisms had again invaded the nation—a
religion, corresponding, for the mass, to what
Goethe's and Kant's philosophy, which is neither
materialism nor spiritualism, is for the few—a
religion based on feeling and intuition, on conscience and reverence, but a religion without
dogmas, without ritual, without forms, above all
without exclusiveness, and without intolerance.
I doubt whether this mild and noble spirit, which
is by no means indifferentism, will soon revive, as
I doubt whether Germany will quickly get over
the conflict between the traditional and the
rationalistic spirit, which mars her public life,
whether too she will soon reach that political
ideal which England realised most fully in the
first half of this century and which consists in a
perfect equilibrium between the spirit of tradition and that of rationalism. However, although
Kant's lofty and Goethe's deep philosophy of life
is now the treasure of a small minority only, it
has none the less pervaded all the great scientific
and literary work done up to the middle of this
century. It has presided over the birth of our new
State; and the day will certainly come when
public opinion in Germany will turn away from
the tendency of her present literature, science, and

politics—a somewhat narrow patriotism, a rather
shallow materialism, and a thoroughly false parliamentary *régime*—and come back to the spirit of
the generations to whom, after all, she owes her
intellectual, though not perhaps her political and
material, civilisation. But I have wandered away
from our immediate subject, and it is time that
I should come back to it, and especially to Kant,
who, at the period we speak of, wielded, with
Goethe and Schiller, the sceptre of intellectual life.

Whoever has studied the history of German
philosophy, knows that there are two Kants; nay,
Kant, I might even say, three Kants. The first
b. 1724. Kant, the young Kant of thirty, started,
as we have seen, from Newton and Rousseau, and
came to a view of the world and of mankind very
much akin to that of Lessing. He was little
noticed then, however, and acted little upon his
contemporaries at large, in spite of the animated,
sometimes even elegant and ornamented, style of
his youthful essays. The second Kant, if I might
be allowed to say so, wrote when he was fifty and
published in 1781 the ' Critic of Pure Reason,' the
most wonderful effort of abstract thought which
the world has seen. By this extraordinary performance Kant effected for the intellectual world,

as he said himself, what Copernicus had effected
for the physical world: an entire change of the
basis of all philosophical study. Before him the
only paths tried in metaphysics were dogmatism
and scepticism. He had himself followed first the
one with Leibnitz-Wolff; then the other with
Hume; but coming to no satisfactory conclusion
with either, he at last chose a third way, the
critical, and made this 'footpath a highroad' to
the knowledge of speculative truth.

Till now it was taken for granted that our understanding must accommodate itself to the objects; but all
attempts to learn anything which might widen our knowledge by *a priori* conceptions were without result in
consequence of that supposition. Let us try, therefore,
whether we do not come nearer to the solution of metaphysical problems, by supposing that objects must accommodate themselves to our understanding. . . . It is with
this as with the first thought of Copernicus. Not succeeding with the explanation of the celestial movements
as long as he supposed that all the host of stars turned
round the observer, he tried whether he would not
succeed better if he left the stars quiet, and made the
observer turn round.

There can be no doubt that the hypothesis
proved true in both cases. Kant's philosophy
is to the metaphysics before him what astronomy

is to astrology, what chemistry is to alchymy.
As he proclaimed, he achieved the momentous
revolution by submitting to examination the instrument itself of philosophising, *i.e.* human
reason, for, according to him, philosophy is a
science which treats ' of the limits of reason,' and
he showed why it is incapable of grasping the infinite in space and time, as well as the idea of a first
cause. Space, indeed, as well as time, and indirectly causality, are not qualities of the outer
world, but laws of our mind, or rather ' forms of
our representation,' which have nothing to do with
the things themselves. In fact, objects of the
senses can never be known, but as they *appear* to
us (through the subjective medium of space and
time) not as they *are* in themselves; and objects
which our senses do not perceive are no objects
for our theoretical knowledge. (Remark the *theoretical*, because on it the later evolution of Kant
hinges.) Kant never denied the existence of the
sensual world, as Berkeley did; he only contended that we see it not as it is, but as the
forms of our intellect make it appear. Teleology
is therefore a ' regulative ' principle of our understanding, which supplies a motive for the world of
phenomena, not a ' constitutive ' principle of this
objective world. It is true that Kant added in the

first edition of his book a passage which he left out
in the second, and in which he said, quite in passing, that the 'thing in itself' and the perceiving *ego*
might be one and the same thinking substance, and
it is on this passing hypothesis that 'the three great
impostors,' as Schopenhauer most unjustly calls
Fichte, Schelling, and Hegel, constructed their
whole idealism. Kant himself says plainly
enough :—

> The proposition of all the true idealists, from the
> Eleatic school down to Bishop Berkeley, is contained in
> the formula : all knowledge through the senses and ex-
> perience is mere appearance; truth is only in the ideas
> of pure intelligence and pure reason. The principle
> which governs and pervades all *my* idealism is, on the
> contrary : all knowledge of things through pure intelli-
> gence and pure reason is nothing but appearance; truth
> is only in experience.

All psychology, cosmology, and theology based
on pure reason fall with that principle; for they
are attempts to apply the forms or categories of
the understanding to the 'thing in itself,' which
those very categories prevent it from perceiving,
consequently they *must* mislead. Psychology,
which treats the soul as a thinking substance,
must lead to paralogisms, such as liberty without
motives; theology, with its famous three proofs

of the Deity, deals with empty conceptions ; cosmology, which considers the world as it appears to us, to be the world as it really is, can only end in contradiction or antinomies (*e.g.* the world has a beginning and is limited in space, and the antithesis, the world is eternal and infinite).

The 'Critic of Pure Reason' made a great stir ; but the salutary influence which it

Kant's moral philosophy.

might have exercised at once on the philosophical movement of the country, as it begins to do just now only, was marred to a certain extent by the second great book of Kant, the 'Critic of Practical Reason,' which virtually was a retractation of the first book. Indeed, Fichte, Schelling, Hegel, the so-called continuators of Kant, meant to be true Kantians, when with one foot they stood on the 'Pure Reason,' with the other on the 'Practical Reason.' We all know what was the result of their acrobatic efforts at equilibrium. Schopenhauer, the only thinker who held fast by Kant's great discovery, and took his starting-point from it, combining it at the same time with the Herder-Goethe idea of the ever-working creative power in nature, remained ignored for forty years. Since then there has been a revival of Kant's philosophy, which will, I trust,

prove permanent; and it is particularly remarkable that, as Kant started from the natural sciences
to arrive at the criticism of the mind, so his
critical method has in our days penetrated into,
and pervades, all the natural sciences. Almost
all the really great men of science in Germany are
neither materialists nor spiritualists, nor sceptics,
but critics, if I may say so, of the Kantian school.
This, however, is not the place to enter further
into an exposition of Kant's ' Pure Reason ; ' for
here, I repeat, we are not studying the history of
philosophy any more than that of literature and
the State, but the history of the general thought
of the German nation. Now a book like Kant's
' Pure Reason ' cannot exercise any direct influence on the general thought of a nation ; it is
too special for that, too difficult, too abstract;
it remains the esoteric property of the philosophers. Even the indirect influence which it
must exercise, the exoteric doctrine, which belongs
to the domain of these lectures, begins only to
be felt in our days, as I said just now, and we
are speaking here of the end of the past century.
Not so with what I venture to call the third
Kant. Kant published his ' Critic of Practical
Reason ' in 1788, his ' Critic of Judgment ' in 1790,

and 'these two books had a deep and immediate
effect on general thought. Schiller modified his
æsthetic views under the influence of the latter,
and the best of a whole generation lived and
acted in the lofty—for us too lofty—moral ideas
of the former.

Kant's 'Critic of Pure Reason' had been the
scientific analysis of the human intellect. His
'Critic of Practical Reason' may be regarded as
the scientific analysis of human will (or, more
exactly, desire), together with a reconstruction of
the metaphysical world through moral feeling.
Kant, indeed, contended that there were only
three psychological faculties : understanding,
volition, and feeling. Understanding contains
its own principles and those of the other two.
Considered with regard to its own principles, it is
'Pure Reason ; ' considered with regard to volition,
it is 'Practical Reason;' considered with regard to
the feeling of pleasure and pain, it is 'Judgment.'
Now, Kant contends that there is a sentiment of
morality inborn in us, and he calls it, in opposition
to all conditional morality, the 'categoric imperative,' which orders us to act so or so. We have it,
he contends, without and before experience, and it
tells us what is right and wrong independently of

all the dictates of a given social law in a given period or nation. Liberty consists in our obeying this inner law. He had himself stated that this is an idea which cannot be proved, that for reason liberty does not and cannot exist; but it exists, he now urges, for feeling; and· as he had shown in his 'Pure Reason' that behind this experimental and phenomenal world there might be a different world superior to, or rather exterior to, the laws of our understanding and senses, so this undoubted feeling of a moral law within us proves that this possible higher world really exists. This is the *monstrum*, to use Schopenhauer's words, to which Kant found his way: 'a theoretical doctrine' which is theoretically indefensible, and which has only practical value!

From this postulate, then, Kant reconstructs the immortality of the soul, as the necessary condition for realising our inborn ideal of virtue, and the personal Deity as being a consequence of our inborn desire of happiness; in other words, the very things which in his 'Pure Reason' he had proved to be unprovable. 'We can imagine,' he then said of the Deity plausibly enough, 'an intelligence which, not being discursive like ours, but intuitive, might go from the general to the

particular . . . ;' but for *us*, men, there is no
knowledge except through the combination of
sensation with the forms and categories of the
intelligence. There is no faculty within us to
create anything without materials furnished by
the senses. Consequently the particulars furnished
by the senses on one side, and the unity which
we impart to them by our combining intellect on
the other side, would remain independent of each
other. If they correspond, it might be mere
chance ; it is only by supposing a divine mind
really intuitive that this casual, accidental cor-
respondence would become a necessary identity.
But this, he surmises (and with him all thinkers
who wish to remain within the limits assigned by
Kant himself to human intelligence), would always
remain an hypothesis. Now, in his 'Practical
Reason,' this hypothesis suddenly becomes a
reality, through the inner sense of the moral
law. Once more, in his third great work, to
which we shall revert by and by, in the 'Critic
of Judgment,' Kant destroys the old onto-
logical, cosmological, and physico-theological
proofs of the existence of a personal God,
only to admit the *moral* proof—not before
the tribunal of Reason, of course, but on the

ground of sentiment, and before that of practical necessity.

Kant's whole religion, however, is always founded upon the moral law alone, not upon reason and argument like that of the rationalists and Deists; still less upon individual revelation, like that of the mystics and pietists; least of all on the Bible or tradition, like that of the orthodox and theologians.

Men *will* not understand (he says) that when they fulfil their duties to men, they fulfil thereby God's commandments; that they are consequently always in the service of God, as long as their actions are moral, and that it is absolutely impossible to serve God otherwise.

And again :

As everybody likes to be honoured, so people imagine that God also wants to be honoured. They forget that the fulfilment of duty towards men is the only honour adequate to him. Thus is formed the conception of a religion of worship, instead of a merely moral religion. . . . Apart from moral conduct, all that man thinks himself able to do in order to become acceptable to God is mere superstition and religious folly. If once a man has come to the idea of a service which is not purely moral, but is supposed to be agreeable to God himself, or capable of propitiating him, there is little difference between the several ways of serving him. For all these ways are of

equal value. . . . Whether the devotee accomplishes his
statutory walk to the church, or whether he undertakes
a pilgrimage to the sanctuaries of Loretto and Palestine,
whether he repeats his prayer-formulas with his lips, or
like the Tibetan, uses a prayer-wheel . . . is quite
indifferent. As the illusion of thinking that a man can
justify himself before God in any way by acts of worship
is religious superstition, so the illusion that he can
obtain this justification by the so-called intercourse with
God is religious mysticism (*Schwärmerei*). Such superstition leads inevitably to sacerdotalism (*Pfaffenthum*)
which will always be found where the essence is sought
not in principles of morality, but in statutory commandments, rules of faith and observances.

The last consequence of Kant's principle is
that religion should be

. . . . successively freed from all statutes based on history,
and one purely moral religion rule over all, in order that
God might be all in all. The veil must fall. The leading-
string of sacred tradition with all its appendices . . .
becomes by degrees useless, and at last a fetter . . . The
humiliating difference between laymen and clergymen
must disappear, and equality spring from true liberty.
All this, however, must not be expected from an exterior
revolution, which acts violently, and depends upon
fortune. In the principle of pure moral religion, which
is a sort of divine revelation constantly taking place in
the soul of man, must be sought the ground for a passage
to the new order of things, which will be accomplished
by slow and successive reforms.

And as in religion so in the State; with the difference that he not only wanted to break with all tradition, but wished also to see the new State founded on purely rational prin- Kant's political views. ciples. Hence his enthusiasm for the North-American Republic and for the French Revolution, in spite of his previous conviction that 'a revolution might bring about the downfall of personal despotism and avaricious oppression, but never a true reform . . . for new prejudices would serve as well as the old for leading-strings for the thoughtless mass' (1785). When, in 1792, the Republic was proclaimed, he said with tears in his eyes: 'Now, I can say like Simeon, Lord, now lettest Thou Thy servant depart in peace, for mine eyes have seen Thy salvation.' He was somewhat shaken by the death of Louis XVI., some months later, and wrote once more (1793) against the right of rebellion; but soon after the reign of terror was over, and even during the Directory, when everybody turned away in disgust, he remained faithful to his belief, that the French Revolution was the dawn of a new day for mankind, the first great attempt to found a State on reason alone. We must not allow ourselves to be misled by his polemic against Rousseau's 'Contrat social.'

P

Here, as in his metaphysics, he drew the distinction between theoretical and practical truth, contending that *in fact* there was nothing like a contract, either between all the members of a nation, or between the citizens and the king. His political views remained nevertheless in their essence those of the constitution-mongers of the century, from Montesquieu to Hamilton. In this he remained isolated in Germany. The incredible and universal enthusiasm which the Revolution had excited there gave way to very different feelings after the execution of the King; and even the principle of a rational constitution was soon abandoned for the more congenial idea of progress through a reform of the traditional institutions. It was Burke, the English Herder, who became the prophet of the rising generation in Germany.

Not so with Kant's religious and moral ideas. The former found a most eloquent interpreter in Schleiermacher, and it was, I might say, the national religion during almost half a century. The moral principle, on which Kant based his religion, Kant's made, indeed, an immediate impression in influence. spite of its almost superhuman severity. When Kant proclaimed this stern idea of inexor-

able duty, the German world was practically and
theoretically worshipping selfishness, be it under
the form of indulgence to caprice, or under that
of meek sentimentality, while Courts vied with
literary circles in ' *genial* ' license. Kant's was a
morality not of passion or disposition, but of firm
principles and severe commandments. Love and
affection are in his eyes no more moral motives
than utility and ambition. The one motive is:
' thou shalt '; fulfilment of duty for duty's sake,
respect for the unbending moral law. When he
preached absolute political liberty, equality, and
self-government, the German nation still lived
under the most arbitrary despotism of three hundred absolute rulers; it was divided into narrow
castes, and no public life existed. When he called
for a peaceful federation of all civilised nations,
(1795) a war which seemed destined never to end
was still raging almost throughout Europe. It
was, perhaps, this contrast of his ideas with the
surrounding world which gave them such power
over men's minds. There can be no doubt that the
generation of Stein and Scharnhorst, of Fichte and
Arndt, was fed and inspired with Kant's moral
views, that they obeyed his ' categoric imperative,'
when they withstood violence and injustice, when

they chose exile and privation rather than wrong their conscience, when they rose at last against the foreign oppressor, but only after having given to their own countrymen liberty, equality and, as far as the times would allow, self-government. You all know that Stein abolished the last remnants of serfdom, made the soil free, and gave the cities their autonomy, whilst Scharnhorst introduced that palladium of our revived nation, equal military service for every citizen whether rich or poor, nobleman or peasant, and created that army, which, even should it ever become superfluous for the defence of national independence, should it ever cost us twice as much as it does, will be maintained as that national high school of unselfishness, reverence, manliness, and true idealism which it has been for the last seventy years, in the silent times of universal peace, still more than in the stirring moments of glorious warfare.[1]

---

[1] In general, there is a good deal of exaggeration in the way the English Press speaks of the financial burdens our army imposes upon us. The sum total of the German taxation, direct *and* indirect, amounts to 15s. 2d. per head, whereas that of England is not less than 2l. 0s. 3d. Germany spends $17\frac{1}{2}$ millions annually for military purposes on a total budget of 84 millions, *i.e.* about one fifth; Great Britain spends $32\frac{1}{4}$ millions on a total budget of 128 millions, *i.e.* about one fourth.

Still, I must be allowed to say that Kant's
moral creed was no more *the* German one than his
political *credo*. Even the men of whom I just spoke
were obliged practically to bend its rigid rules and
to adapt them to the exigencies of circumstance and
of character. No, the idea of free will is no more a
German idea than radicalism or rationalism. The
pretension of basing morality on the conception of
duty alone, and without taking into account either
the inborn nobility or meanness of character or pity
and emotion is no more German than is the attempt
to create religion and State, without and in contradiction to the given historical circumstances and
traditions, according to reason and by means of a
conscious will. These are no German ideas, and, as
I am addressing an English audience, I may say
they are not Teutonic ideas. Our culture—yours
still more than ours—has been strongly, and on
the whole healthily, influenced by Pelagianism and
rationalism; still, at the root it has remained
faithful to Augustinianism as to the belief in
the unconsciously working powers of history and
nature, and in the *rights* of these powers. A true
Teutonic mind will certainly never admit that history is only a long series of unmeaning accidents;
but still less will it admit that the traditional

state which we have inherited from our forefathers is only a heap of abuses and absurdities wilfully introduced, and to be done away with entirely
in order to make room for constitutions, framed
by abstract reason and for abstract men. It will
never admit that religion is only an imposture of
priests and a tissue of superstitions, to be replaced
by an enlightened system of morality, and that
the poor in spirit should be denied the right to
satisfy *his* craving for an ideal by giving to this,
his ideal, a palpable, or at least a sentimental
form. It will never admit that morality is to be
sought only in obedience to the commandment
of duty, that such a thing as life for high disinterested pursuits, like science and art, such
a thing as generous and even unwise impulse,
such a thing as pity, above all, and instinctive
self-sacrifice, should not constitute morality as
well as the obedience to duty. It will never
admit that men are free and equal morally.
When, at the great revolt of the Teutonic spirit
against the Latin, which we call the Reformation,
Luther placed faith above works and claimed the
privilege of salvation for the elect, was he not ex-
pressing in his language the same thought which,
two centuries later, was put into words by the

second great Teutonic rebel against the Latin
spirit, Herder, when he said that the man living
in the ideal could not be immoral; or by his
disciple *malgré lui*, Fr. Schlegel, when he spoke
of the moral aristocracy of 'noble natures' (*Edel-
gebornen*); or by Schleiermacher, when he gave a
new form to the doctrine of St. Augustin? Did
he not give the form of his time, *i.e.* the theological, to the fundamental conception of a Shakespeare, a Fielding, and a Goethe, when they
showed us their Prince Hal, their Tom Jones,
their Egmont, as noble, sympathetic, and elect
natures, in spite of their freaks, their follies, and
their sins?

Besides, it was not Herder alone who remonstrated against Kant's ideas of morality, Schiller, b.
politics, and religion, as against his whole 1759.
way of analysing what in nature is united. Schiller
himself, Kant's greatest disciple, has lent to his
'Wallenstein' the finest words in which ever the
true Teutonic idea, from Luther down to Schopenhauer, the negation of absolute free will, was
formulated:

> Hab' ich des Menschen Kern erst untersucht,
> So kenn' ich auch sein Wollen und sein Handeln, &c.

Schiller, it is true, does not speak these words in

his own name; he puts them into the mouth of his fatalistic hero. Nay, he always insists upon freedom as the distinctive quality of man in opposition to necessity, which is the law of nature; but he always means by it the *co-operation* of intellectual and moral motives in the formation of our actions, not the absolute rule of those motives. In this, as in all the rest, he extenuated the rigidity of Kant's doctrines, and largely modified at last what he had taken from Kant. Was it not Schiller himself who wrote the famous epigram against Kant's categoric imperative?

Willingly I serve my friends; unfortunately I do it with pleasure, and so I am often angry with myself for not being virtuous. There is only one remedy: try to despise your friends, and then do with horror what duty commands.

Already before studying Kant's great works, Schiller had arrived at the same conclusions as Kant with regard to history. Starting from Rousseau, as Herder, and Kant himself in his earlier works, had done, he had contended that the state of nature, so much vaunted by Jean Jacques, was reconcilable with civilisation, provided this civilisation was a simple one like that of the Greeks, which, far from stifling natural

spontaneousness as ours does, develops it. The
aim of Humanity was to be Nature purified by
culture. The prototype of this renovated and
ennobled nature was the Hellenic world. Here
you have almost literally Kant's earlier ideas
of 1764. Nevertheless, Schiller already goes his
own way even here, when he sees in Art the
first civilising power which prepares moral and
scientific culture, as well as the crowning of all
civilisation, the highest development of man.
The ideal of mankind, in his eyes, will be attained
only when moral and scientific culture is placed
again under the principle of beauty, in other
words, when life itself becomes again a work of
art, as it was in Greece.

When, after having put forth this view in
1789, in his great poem, ' The Artists,' he made
the acquaintance of Kant's works, Schiller was
exceedingly struck and even conquered by them;
but soon a reaction took place, and he tried to complete and modify Kant's moral doctrine, in order to
bring it into harmony with his own artistic propensities and predilections. Kant's condemnation
of the senses, his rigid conception of duty, hurt
the artistic nature of Schiller, who endeavoured to
show that moral beauty, not moral actions, ought

to be the ideal aim of man, because perfection could only be attained when duty had become a second nature to man. Already, in his æsthetic treatises, Schiller had contended against Kant that beauty was not only a subjective sensation, but that it existed objectively in things. As often as an object is, what it is, by itself and for itself, it is beautiful, according to him—an idea already contained, however, in Kant's 'teleologic' or objective judgment, as opposed to the 'æsthetic' or subjective judgment, although Schiller corrected Kant's conception of a higher teleology by that of autonomy. This objective beauty—a most doubtful conception—Schiller called architectural beauty, and he opposed to it the moveable beauty or grace, which belongs only to free beings, and which is the expression of the beautiful soul regulating all the movements of the body. Architectural beauty, he says, does honour to the Author of nature, moveable beauty to the possessor, who is at the same time its creator.

Now, what is the state of the soul which produces this moveable beauty or grace? It cannot be the absolute empire of reason over the senses, because the liberty of nature is impaired thereby; it cannot be the absolute rule of the senses, which are always under the yoke of necessity. Hence, beauty of soul exists, when both come to a kind of mixed constitution and compromise, in which reason and sense, duty and inclination, coincide. Man is designed not for the performance of particular moral actions, but to be a moral being. His perfection lies not in virtues, but virtue; and virtue is only inclination for duty. 'We call a soul beautiful, when the moral feeling has become so thoroughly master of all the sensations of man that he can without fear abandon to impulse the direction of the will.' Thence, in a beautiful soul, it is not the particular actions which are moral; the whole character is moral. This, you see, is a reconciliation of the Herderian and Kantian ideas by the evocation of the Hellenic ideal; it is the serene *Kalokagathia* of the Greeks, not Kant's rigid law of the categoric imperative, which treats the senses like slaves.

This ideal of the beautiful soul, however, is practically almost unattainable. There are moments when the assaults of the senses must be conquered; and these moments will be the test whether the moral beauty is really an acquired possession which will resist, or only an inborn disposition to kindness and a goodness of tempera-

ment which will give way. If it is the former, the
victory will be dignity, which is not the opposition,
but the completion of grace; for 'grace lies in the
freedom of our voluntary movements, dignity in the
rule over involuntary movements.' I need scarcely
say that I am here simply stating the ideas of the
great German thinkers and poets. I do not discuss
them. I also adopt their terminology, even when
it seems to me objectionable, as that of Schiller
when he uses the words dignity, grace, beauty.
The means, according to Schiller, to acquire
beauty of soul, are art and science, because they
are the only things in which our personal interest
does not come into question, and in which consequently we are, philosophically speaking, really
free. The contemplation of nature and its forms,
and the study thereof, without a wish to possess,
utilise, or enjoy the objects of such contemplation
or study for our personal advantage, constitute
art and science.

The ideal of a human society would in consequence be a sort of æsthetic community, which
Schiller, however, was quite resigned not to see
ever realised, except in some select sphere.
Nevertheless, he thinks that the example of Greece
shows that the thing is possible. Whilst with us

there is nothing but barbarism on one side, corruption on the other, and a division of labour everywhere, with the Greeks there was nature *and* culture; their work was not divided, nor were their souls. Thucydides was, at the same time, a philosopher, a physician, an admiral, a statesman, and an historian; and Xenophon, the naturalist, showed himself a great general when circumstances required it. Something analogous must be done for the modern world. All political amendment, however, must proceed from an amendment of character. For this we want an instrument independent of the State, an instrument which the general corruption will not touch; and this instrument is art. Each of us must, somewhat in the spirit of Goethe's *Wilhelm Meister*, try to educate himself, to make of himself a beautiful soul, to develop all the germs of his individuality to an harmonious unity. Thus Schiller, by the philosophical way, reaches the same goal which Herder had reached by the study of history, and Goethe by the study of nature—I mean, the ideal of humanism. The completion of Schiller's ideas his friend, W. von Humboldt, gave in his strange book on the 'Limits of the Action of the State,' which reads like a chapter of J. S. Mill's 'Essay on

Liberty' from an idealistic, instead of from an utilitarian, point of view: for W. von Humboldt wants to see the power and interference of the State limited to the utmost, only in order that the freest and most harmonious development of individuality may not be impeded.

Thus the emancipative tendencies of the century, which elsewhere had led to the democratic conclusion of the superior rights of individual reason over collective wisdom as represented by tradition, of common sense over genius, and thence to affirming the equal value of all individuals, led in Germany to the aristocratic view of the recognition of superior individualities and their rights, and thence to considering the education of these individualities (not the satisfaction of the interests, passions, and wishes of the greater number) as the means and aim of civilisation. It is but natural that the former view should favour the development of utilitarianism and of positive science, and that the latter should generate the artistic and the historical treatment of things.

There is no doubt that Schiller definitively determined the province of art, when he said that it consisted not in dreaming of an unreal, fantastic world, but in discerning the ideal in the real world, in seeing in the accidental the manifestation of the eternal. The question is whether he and his time were right in seeing the dignity of man preserved in art alone, because in art alone man was free and active, his own master, and yet working upon the outer world. A second and secondary question is whether they did not entirely misunderstand Greece, where State and City formed the basis of the whole national existence and by no means only a disagreeable necessity. Finally, there is always the Mephistophelian objection: what, if you had seen Greece near? would you not have found things somewhat different from what they seem to you in the haze of distance? One thing, however, is certain: the standpoint of Schiller remained that of the whole age in its greatest representatives. The weak side of it is obvious; and cruel reality stirred up Germany, proving to her harshly enough that the much despised State was the necessary ground upon which alone man could devote himself with dignity and security to his æsthetic perfection.

Things have been reversed since then in Germany. The idea of the State, so utterly obliterated in Schiller's time, has become exceedingly active and powerful; and the nation is eager

to sacrifice everything to it. Schiller's idea is not
extinct for all that. As long as the national State,

*Present
views on
State.*
the lack of which had been so painfully
felt in the moment of need, is being constructed, it is natural that the nation
should show a certain onesidedness and exclusiveness in this direction. For the time being, individualism, as preached by the great pathfinders of
German culture, seems almost vanished. The
nation in which Madame de Staël did not find
two minds thinking alike on any subject, has
become singularly gregarious, nay, uniform; the
great producer and consumer of original ideas is
content nowadays to feed on some few watchwords
mechanically repeated. Individualism indeed,
humanism, absence of prejudice and of social conventionality, when pushed so far as they were by
the generation of Schiller and Goethe, are absolute
hindrances to public life, which subsists only by
the sacrifice of individual interests and convictions to party principles or national interests. A
nation, or a class, or a party in a nation, is irresistible only when it has a whole set of common
thoughts, interests, feelings, and forms. As long
as each unit goes its own way, nation, class, party
exist only in words, and cannot resist the slightest

shock.   Modern German history proves it on every
page.

And not only has individualism made room for
uniformity, humanism for patriotism, but Schiller's
conception itself that art was the highest form of
human activity, that accidental practical life
must be subordinated to a higher ideal life, has,
as it were, disappeared, for the time being at least.
For I feel confident that, as soon as the long-
yearned-for national State is complete and insured
against inner and outer enemies, Germany will
come back to the creed of the real founders of her
civilisation.   But she will only accept it with quali-
fications.   She will never again profess that un-
spoken contempt for the State, which lay at the
root of all the thought of Schiller's generation;
but neither will she any longer see in the State
an end, as she does now, instead of a means,
a necessary means, a noble means even, but a
means, nevertheless, not an end.   It seems impossible, indeed, that the nation of Lessing and
Herder, Goethe and Kant, should not weary of
politics as she wearied, long ago, of theology, and,
leaving politics to the politicians as she left theology to the theologians, should not set to work

Q

again at the ideal content of life, instead of at
the containing forms.

There is no contradiction in this, as might
at first sight appear. If there are domains of
human activity, where absolute individualism is
an evil, and a sign of selfishness, there are others
where it is as fertile as it is noble. And so it is
with collectivism, if I may use that term. A
blessing in one department of life, it is a curse in
the other. But is it really impossible to confine
each of them within limits which will render it
salutary? The Germany of 1800 knew only individualism; the Germany of 1879 seems to know
only collectivism. The Germany of the future, let
us hope, will submit to collectivism, and will be
ready to sacrifice individual thought and feeling
where it is necessary to do so, *i.e.* in State and
society. She will claim full liberty of personal
thought and feeling, where individualism alone
can bear fruit, *i.e.* in art and science; and in
doing so she will feel that she has chosen the
better part: for he, who tries to penetrate the
world—humanity and nature—and to interpret it
faithfully and lovingly, be it by the artist's intuition and second creation, be it by the intellect and
learning of the scholar, has chosen a higher

activity than the man who lives only in and for the State and its passing interests.

We shall see, however, in the next and last of these lectures, how the contrary conviction was brought about in Germany, and what is its justification.

LECTURE VI.

THE ROMANTIC SCHOOL.

1800—1825.

WE have seen that the great task of giving to
Germany the foundations of a new and national
culture fell to three generations, that of Winckelmann, Kant, and Lessing ; that of Herder, Goethe,
and Schiller ; that of the two Schlegels and the two
Humboldts, which was also that of Hardenberg
and Tieck, of Rahel and Gentz, of Schelling and
Hegel, of Arndt and Kleist, of Schleiermacher and
Hölderlin, not to speak of many other less celebrated writers and thinkers who were all born
towards the year 1770. It is of this generation,
whose principal works were published from 1800
to 1815, that I have to speak to you to-day. My
remarks must be, if possible, of a character still
more summary and, I am afraid, more superficial
than those I have presented to you thus far, as

this is our last meeting, and I wish also to notice rapidly, as in an epilogue, the different currents of thought which have agitated Germany during the quarter of a century succeeding the palmy days of the romantic school, which forms the main subject of the present lecture.

The romanticists were by no means from the first day such as they appear to us now, and such as they will figure for ever in the history of thought. They also, like the two preceding generations, fought their battle on the literary field, the only one then open to Germany ; and they began only later to act upon the public life of their country. When they first began to attract attention, they gave themselves out as staunch admirers of Goethe, and adhered strictly to Schiller's principles. It was only in their second phase of development that they turned round against the reigning classicism.

The Starting-point.

Two things are necessary for the poet and artist (says Schiller) ; he must rise above reality, and he must remain within the sensuous. Where both those exigencies are fulfilled equally, there is æsthetic art. But in an unfavourable and shapeless nature (and society), he too easily abandons the sensuous along with the real, and becomes idealistic, and, if his understanding be feeble, even fantastic; or when he wishes, and is obliged by his nature, to remain in the sensuous, he obstinately clings to the real, and becomes realistic in the narrow sense of the word, and even servile and vulgar if he wholly lacks imagination. In both cases he is not æsthetic.

These golden words, which the artist and poet can never meditate upon sufficiently, or keep too steadily before his mind, found a notable commentary in the German literature of the time. Whilst Goethe and Schiller were on the limit, and often even overstepped the limit, which separates artistic truth—or what they called æsthetic beauty—from abstract idealism, there were many writers who were pleased to dwell within the most vulgar, everyday reality, because they were either afraid or unable to rise into ideal regions. And these writers had a far more numerous public than our classics. The Ifflands, Schröders, Kotzebues, Aug. Lafontaines, and others were in possession of the stage, and made the fortune of the circulating libraries. The prosiest philistine-life became the object of literature, and the inartistic forms of this life were reproduced in poetry, if not yet by plastic art. Schiller and Goethe declared pitiless war against this vulgarity; and it was no wonder if they exaggerated on their side, not only by the

occasional misuse of the weapon of satire, but also
by the example of their works. In the beginning
of their classical period, which is that of their
maturity, they had still taken their subjects and
their inspiration from real life and national history.
'Hermann and Dorothea' and 'Wallenstein'
are in the highest degree what Schiller required
works of art to be, 'within the limits of the
sensuous, but raised above accidental reality.' So
in spite of the foreign costume were 'Tasso' and
'Iphigenia,' 'Egmont' and the 'Roman Elegies.'
They showed reality, *i.e.* concrete feelings
and passions, personages and situations, reduced
to their eternal, artistic element, and thereby
interpreted reality by art. More than this,
'Wilhelm Meister' had shown that the task of
life, the task of the time particularly in which
Goethe lived, was to recognise the rights of reality,
and to reconcile idealism with this reality. When
once the battle had begun against the vulgar
realists, who thought a button-hole an object as
worthy of art as a human face, and a wart on
that face as important as the lines of the forehead,
Goethe and Schiller were led to the same extreme
to which the Fine Arts had already been drifting.
In their horror of prosy reality they fled into the

classic world of antiquity and even into abstract
idealism ; and just as Carstens and David looked
for ideal types, and thought to find them in the
art of the ancients alone, so they began to give
classic names and forms to mental abstractions,
turned the old gods which Herder had shown to
be living mythical individualities once more into
lifeless symbols of general conceptions, and fell
again into full allegory.   If they were not entirely
lost in it, it was because the ideas they allegorised
were of real depth, and because their artistic
genius was so powerful that even allegory lost
something of its inanimate coldness under their
hands. 'Pandora' and 'Paleophron and Euterpe'
are still read, in spite, not because, of the æsthetic
theory which was godmother to them.   The pretext for thus abandoning the 'sensuous' was not
even plausible.   The German life of their time,
they said, offered no fit objects for poetry.   'Hermann and Dorothea' is the most eloquent refutation of that paradox, if it wanted refutation.
Men's costume may sometimes be inartistic ; their
body and soul is never entirely devoid of interest
for the artist, although it may offer to him a
more or less fertile object.

The young romanticists went a step further

still than Schiller and Goethe, who had become—
for the time being, at least—one-sided idealists;
'they became dreamers because their understanding was feeble.' Goethe and Schiller, indeed, even
when they went so far as to seek their subjects
beyond the bounds of reality, in abstract thought
or a so-called ideal world, at least treated them
with the wisdom of artistic understanding and in
an objective way. Their young disciples and allies
deemed their caprice and inspiration sufficient
guides, and treated their imaginary themes in a
quite subjective manner. So, strangely enough, it
came to pass that they took from Goethe and
Schiller just the shortcomings of their youthful as
well as of their mature age, and disdained the
superior qualities which distinguished them in
both periods. In their youth the two great poets
had sought in reality and personal experience the
materials of their poetry, treating them, however,
with a 'subjectivity' which did not recognise the
authority of artistic understanding as the regulating power. Fifteen years later they came to the
conviction that no great work of art can be produced without that regulating power, but, disgusted
with the realistic literature of the time, they sought
their objects outside reality. In this the young

romanticists followed them, but remained in the
other respect at the point where their masters
had been in the 'Sturm- und Drangperiode';
they recognised no right of control by the understanding. The only controlling power they admitted was irony, *i.e.* reason, hovering over and
smiling at the work done by unfettered fancy.
The consequence was that they, without the
guidance of artistic understanding, soon went still
farther astray than their models, and not only fled
from the surrounding reality, like Goethe and
Schiller, but from all reality, into the world of
mere imagination. Even to such creations, however, they did not know how to give plastic, sensuous, palpable form ; all remains musical, lyrical,
vague, subjective, like their inspiration. They
pride themselves on this personal character of both
object and form in their poetry. They transferred
to art the philosophic system of Fichte, for whom
the whole universe was only the production of the
Ego; and the one activity of this *Ego*, which they
recognised as the supreme, was Imagination,
fantasy. They soon felt the complete contradiction between themselves and the classical
Hellenic world, evoked by Schiller and Goethe, and
opposed to it the world of the middle ages, whose

chiaroscuro is infinitely more favourable to their dreamy, fantastic art; and they ended with trying practically to restore the middle ages in order to get a poetical reality. The apostles of unlimited personal liberty in art and life became the missionaries of a religious and political conservatism, which would erase from history three centuries of progressive enlightenment, because the preachers of such conservatism feel more comfortable in the dark than in daylight.

German romanticism, you see, is totally different from that which the French have since called by this name, and which bears infinitely more resemblance to the principles of the German 'Sturm- und Drangperiode,' viz., the emancipation from all æsthetic rules. For the French, for instance, Shakespeare's 'Coriolanus' would be a romantic drama, Corneille's 'Cid' a classical one. It is just the reverse with the Germans. The form of the 'Cid,' of 'Polyeucte,' may be classical, the inspiration is modern, *i.e.* subjective, and the process of creation is modern, *i.e.* conscious. The form of 'Julius Cæsar' 'may be ever so different from Sophocles,' the inspiration is objective, the process of creation *naïf*, as with the ancients. Now German roman-

Definition of romanticism.

ticism was, above all, a reaction in favour of
imagination and faith against the enlightenment
and rationalism of the preceding age, but also a
reaction in favour of Christianity and the middle
ages against the Hellenic heathendom of the end
of the century. The theorist of the school, the
younger Schlegel, defined it in these words :

Romanticism rests solely on Christianity and the feeling of charity and love which, thanks to this religion,
reigns also in poetry. In this feeling, suffering itself
appears as a means of glorification and transfiguration.
The traditions of the Greek, Germanic, and Scandinavian
mythology become in it graceful and serene plays of the
imagination. Even among the external forms of style and
language, the romantic poet chooses those which answer
best to this intimate feeling of love, and those plays of
the imagination.

Love then, sentimental love, fancy, faith,
chivalry, honour, were to be the inspiration of
romantic poetry. And as unity reigned in the
middle ages, so it was to reign again, unity
between head and heart, between poetry, life,
philosophy and religion. 'Romanticism,' said
Fred. Schlegel, 'is the aspiration after an infinite poem, which includes the germs of all other
poems.' And young Novalis : 'Should the funda-

mental laws of imagination really be in opposition to those of logic?' And out-Herdering
Herder: 'Poetical sentiment has something akin
to the sense of divination, to religious sense, even
to madness.' Again, poetry was to be philosophy
without ceasing to be religion for these mystical
minds.

> Philosophy is the hero of poetry (said Novalis). It
> elevates poetry, and shows that it is all in all. . . . The
> separation of poet and philosopher is only apparent and
> injures both; it is the symptom of an illness or of a
> sickly constitution. All ought to centre in the philo-
> sopher who is always omniscient, who *is* the real world *in
> nuce.*

But not philosophy alone, all existence was to
be poetry. Life was to become again poetical, as
they imagined it to have been in the dark ages,
and poetry was to be lived : both poetry and life
under the guidance of religion—not of stern,
prosaic, Protestant, but of warm, coloured, sensuous, Catholic religion.

Thus they overthrew all limits, not only those
which the strong artistic sense of the ancients
had drawn between epic, dramatic, and lyrical
poetry, those which Lessing had laboriously erected
between plastic art and poetry, those which Kant

had sagaciously traced between theoretical and
practical knowledge, but also the limits between
prose and verse, art and life, morality and intellect,
science and religion, imagination and understanding. It was the exaggeration, or rather the
caricature, of Herder's profound principle of unity
—unity and simultaneousness of individual forces
in individual action, of national forces in national
action, of human forces in the pursuit of human
aims. Herder had remonstrated against division
of labour, but only in the sense that a general
basis was required for every special work, that
individual, nation, humanity must be entirely
absorbed in the special work in which they are
engaged. For the romanticists there was no
longer any special work : State, Religion, Science,
Poetry were all one in their eyes. This came in
fact to a denial of all civilisation, whose very
action is specialisation, not indeed of the subjective forces acting, but of the objective mass which
it is its task to master.

No wonder if they saw their ideal in the dark
ages. Where indeed could they find such unity,
poetical life and ' lived ' poetry, political religion
and religious politics, as in the middle ages ?
Novalis went so far as to declare it a misfortune

that the Papacy should no longer have the power
to stop such dangerous theories as those of Copernicus, which made mankind believe itself no longer
the centre and aim of creation.   ' The spirit of all
art and sciences,' said Fred. Schlegel, ' must again
be united in one centre, similar to that which
humanity has lost since the middle ages and to the
restoration of which it must aspire.'   In the words
of his more sober brother, A. William :

Europe was one in those great times.   One chivalry
made friends of all warriors.   All vied in fighting for
one faith.   Hearts were open to one love.   Then also
poetry arose, one in feeling, although different in language.   Now the power of the olden times is gone, and
we dare to speak of them as barbarous !   People have
invented for themselves a narrow wisdom, and what, in
their impotence, they do not understand, they call dreams ;
but nothing which is of a divine nature can thrive any
longer in a time when work is done by unholy hands.
Alas !   This age has neither Faith nor Charity ; how
should it have retained Hope ?

Hence also their antipathy for the Hellenic
world where all is clearness, light and health.
They had begun with masterly studies on Greek
poetry, in F. A. Wolf's sense; had shown great
admiration for Goethe ; had developed Schiller's

theories on sentimental poetry; but in proportion
as they formulated their own principles more
distinctly, they turned against Greek classicism,
as Goethe and Schiller understood it. In their
yearning for twilight, they turned away from a
period when that longed-for unity of life and
poetry was realised in full sunshine, and under
the control of healthy reason. How much more
congenial to them were the dark ages in which
they saw the reign of uncontrolled fantasy, the
outward realisation of their own inner life! If
only they could restore that time, would they not
become the Dantes and Wolframs of their time,
as Goethe and Schiller were the Homers and
Sophocles of theirs? Now, it was particularly
the religion of the Middle Ages which they considered the one higher region, in which all classes,
all cultures and all nations might meet again.
'Art and religion were synonymous' in Z. Werner's
eyes, as poetry and science in Hardenberg's. 'They
made piety,' Goethe says, 'the one foundation of
art, because some monks had been artists, and
consequently all artists ought to be monks;' and
elsewhere he compares them to 'children, who,
to imitate a bell, fasten a rope to a tree and sing
ding-dong, whilst they are moving it.'

To give new life, then, to this bleak, rationalistic age, the spark of imagination was to be
rekindled. Fancy was to become once
more the queen of the world, as they A New Mythology.
imagined she had been in the Middle Ages; and
this sullen, bleak atmosphere was to shine once
more in rich colours and in varied forms. What
was wanting in modern religion as in modern
poetry was a mythology. A mythology then was
to be created anew out of all the fragments of
pagan and German myths, Indian and Christian
legends blent together; the elves and nixes, who
dwelt in the forests and on the rivers, the dwarfs
and kobolds who peopled the mediæval world, were
evoked anew. The fairy tale was to become the
highest form of poetical production, as it was at
once the most simple, and the most composite—the
most simple because it was created by childlike
minds for children; the most composite, as in it
lay united as in a germ, religion and imagination,
poetry and thought, wisdom and folly, legend
and history, in that unity in which they presented
themselves to primitive minds. Even so with the
great geniuses of the Christian era. 'Shakespeare's and Calderon's artistic confusion, the
delightful harmony of contradictions, the wonder-

R

ful alternations of enthusiasm and irony, which show themselves in the smallest fragment, seem a new peculiar kind of mythology ; for the beginning of all poetry is to suspend the processes and laws of speculative reason, and to take us back into the beautiful confusion of imagination, into the primitive chaos of nature.' Heine, a romanticist himself in his earlier days, to whom it was given to realise in his poems, if not in his life, the poetical ideal which lay at the root of all the aspirations and vague definitions of the romanticists, has wonderfully satirised this mixed mythology and poetical chaos of irony and enthusiasm, of fancy and wit, in his 'Atta Troll,' and in what I cannot help considering his finest work, 'the Exiled Gods.'

You will not wonder when I say that this apotheosis of imagination, ' Jupiter's spoiled child,' as the highest intellectual power, degenerated naturally into a species of mysticism. They were for ever seeking after the 'blue flower,' like *Heinrich von Ofterdingen*, the hero of Hardenberg's novel, the 'Wilhelm Meister' of the school. 'What there is highest in the world,' Fred. Schlegel would say, 'can be told only in symbols, precisely because it is unspeakable.' And

Novalis (Hardenberg), alluding to his beloved Middle Ages as the golden age of mankind, says :

It had then become quite a natural thing to consider the most ordinary and the nearest things as miraculous, and what was strange and supernatural as ordinary. In this way daily life itself surrounded man like a wonderful fairy tale, and that region which most men do but guess at—or question—as a distant incomprehensible thing, became his home. It seemed unnatural that the poets should form a separate class of men. To be a poet was in their eyes the proper activity of the human mind.

Nor otherwise Görres, the tribune of the party, when he speaks of the dark ages : ' Faith, love, heroism, were then mingled in one large stream. Then it was that the new garden of poetry blossomed, the Eden of romanticism.'

Unfortunately there was no genuine simplicity in all this, no spontaneousness, nor that sort of second sight which illuminated for Herder all the darkness of early ages. It was the studied simplicity of pedants and bookworms, who tried laboriously by the effort of understanding and will to arrive at the simple, but rich, direct and concrete conceptions which intuition revealed spontaneously and easily to the

Character of the Romanticists.

original and healthy minds of primitive nations, or to robust and undefiled genius in modern times.

Their Religion. So it is even with their religion. Hardenberg excepted, they had all been sceptics in their first youth. It is possible that in England the Evangelical movement may have awakened, at least indirectly, what might, in one sense, be called the English romanticism of this century, in other words, the Tractarian movement and what followed. In Germany it was from the beginning rather in opposition to pietism, than in accordance with it. Schleiermacher himself, who had been brought up in a school of Moravian Brethren, was intellectually emancipated even before he left it. No, Catholicism was to them all only a question of æsthetics, as A. W. Schlegel himself confessed, and as it was in fact also to Chateaubriand. Most of them remained Protestants, even after they had denounced Protestantism as the sin against the Holy Ghost. Hardenberg himself, the Št. John of the mission, a sickly overstrained nature—Hardenberg who had declared that ' Christianity was finished with the Reformation,' who had called Protestantism 'a sacrilegious revolt against Christianity, which exists only in the unity of the visible and universal Church '—Hard-

enberg-Novalis himself, never left, perhaps had not
the time to leave, the Lutheran Church in which he
was born.   True, there were many among them,
who, following Fred. Schlegel's and Zacharias
Werner's example, actually embraced Catholicism;
but their new religion did not prevent them from
enjoying life and its most worldly pleasures just as
before.   They took from Catholicism only what
suited their tastes, its outward plastic forms, its
deep historical value, some dogmas which might be
interpreted as the symbolical expression of their
philosophic convictions, the uncontested authority
which it represented; but they submitted in no
wise to what was in the least severe, or even only
inconvenient to them in the old faith; for they ex-
hibited a marvellous ingenuity in choosing and
appropriating to themselves in every theory,
political, religious, philosophical or æsthetic, just
what was congenial to their tastes and wants, and
in ignoring the rest as if it did not exist.

As their religious, so was their poetical and
moral attitude.   In whatever they do and say
there is something *voulu* and *tendu* as Their
the French would say, and there is no Ethics.
affectation more insupportable than the affectation
of simplicity.   There was an utter want of healthy

and vigorous sensuousness as well as of natural
genius in most of those men who made such a
pretence of having strong impulses where there
was only a perverted imagination, or, at least, a
self-indulgence, which was content to consider
every caprice as an unconquerable passion. The
doctrines of 'Lucinde,' Fred. Schlegel's youthful
novel, a rehabilitation of the flesh and its rights,
were commented upon by his friend Schleiermacher,
a clergyman, not with Rabelais' or Sterne's jovial
sensuousness, which makes us almost forget their
ecclesiastical robes, but with a sort of unctuous
devotion, as if he spoke of a new religion; and
these doctrines were put into practice during their
whole lifetime by such men as Fr. Schlegel, Gentz,
and Zacharias Werner, who carried epicurism to
a kind of *maëstria*. Divorce was no longer that
respectable institution which allows a fetter to
fall off, when it has become intolerable, and
brings to an end the long expiation of a youthful mistake. Divorce in their circle had become
an every-day occurrence. There is an actual
chassez-croisez among them. Tieck's sister is
divorced from her brother's best friend Bernhardi;
Mendelssohn's daughter is divorced from Veit
and marries Fred. Schlegel; A. W. Schlegel's

wife— the most remarkable among the women of
the generation after Rahel—Caroline Schlegel, is
divorced and marries Schelling, who is ten years
younger than she. There is something unhealthy
even in those who do not break deliberately
through the barriers of society: Hölderlin becomes an early prey to insanity, through his
hopeless passion for the mother of his pupils;
Hardenberg cherishes a sentimental love for a
girl of twelve years, and dies an early death, at
the age of twenty-nine, when this child is taken
from him; Schleiermacher has a romantic re-
lation with another clergyman's wife, and ends
by marrying a third friend's widow, for whom
he had entertained an apparently hopeless love;
Kleist commits suicide, together with a not less
morbidly excited lady friend; Tieck, Clemens
Brentano, and Hoffmann made *bizarrerie* a system,
and lived according to that system.

Their moral indifference itself varied widely
from that of a Diderot and his friends. There
was a consciousness about it, which deprived it of
the only excuse to be pleaded for it. When they
contended that ' to have understood a thing was
to have justified it;' when they pleaded that
'noble creatures pay with what they are, not

with what they do'; when they thus brought the
doctrines of election and grace into a worldly system
which had no other aim than to justify their own
loose morals; when these refined Epicureans of
Culture, these impotent dilettanti, who have not
produced a single lasting poem, were for ever
talking of spontaneousness and imagination and
popular simplicity—they were certainly theoretically in the right. But it was plain to everyone
that the thing most wanting in them was the one
they most recommended and praised, whilst, on
the contrary, they most depreciated the faculty
they possessed in the highest degree, that of
criticism.

It was by this faculty nevertheless that they
acted principally on their time and on the follow-
Their
action in
Germany. ing generation. For they acted powerfully upon it, not only in the domain of
poetry and art, but also in that of science and
politics.

It was the romanticists, indeed, who created
modern literary history, of which Herder had only
Their in-
fluence on
Literary
History. sketched the outlines. They collected
the popular songs and fairy tales of Old
Germany; they republished, and commented upon, the poems of Wolfram and Gott-

fried, the 'Nibelungen' and the 'Gudrun;' and
they did it with a delicacy, and a poetical tact,
which have been completely lost, since the literary
history of the Middle Ages has been treated only
from a grammatical point of view.   Nor was it only
the literary history of the German Middle-Age
which the romanticists created; they brought
Dante again to honour and with him all the minor
medieval poets of the South as well as of their own
country.   Their translations of the Renaissance
poets, of Shakespeare particularly, of Bojardo,
Ariosto, Calderon, Camoens, Cervantes, have, it
may be said, made the master-works of the world
the property of the German nation.   It is their
merit if, after such a total change of atmosphere,
and when the worship of foreign things, which
characterised the old Germany, has long subsided,
these masterworks still keep their place on the
German stage and in German libraries beside those
of Goethe, Schiller, and Lessing.   Germany owes
to them not only the naturalisation of the poets
of all latitudes and times ; but also that of the
poetical forms of all nations and periods.   It was
they who introduced and acclimatised the Italian
terzina and canzona, the Spanish *redondilla*, the
Persian *gasela*, as their predecessors had introduced

and acclimatised in German poetry the hexameter
and the alcaic strophe of the Greeks. It was
Fr. Schlegel, who first sought and found in India
the highest expression of romanticism, *i.e.* 'the
deepest and most intimate life of the imagination.
When once we are able to draw from the original
sources, perhaps the appearance of southern glow,
which now attracts us so much in Spanish poetry,
will appear to us but pale and occidental.'

Then, again, their reaction against the exclusive Hellenism of Goethe and Schiller gave impulse
to the new poetry of the national and Christian
type, of which Uhland has remained and will remain
the most charming representative; to the great
national dramas of a Kleist, which after all are
the most effective that Germany has produced
for the stage, if we except those of Lessing and
Schiller; to the patriotic songs of 1813 (the
Schenkendorffs and Arndts, Körners and Rück-
erts, all belonged, more or less, to the romantic
school) to the new fantastic novel-literature of
the Arnims, Brentanos, Hoffmanns, Chamissos,
Fouqués; above all, to what there is best and most
imperishable in Heine's wonderful productions.
I am not giving you here a literary history of
Germany; otherwise I should have to show you the

different ramifications of the romantic school;
the group of the fatalists, that of the patriots, that
of the pure fantasts, that of the sentimentalists,
who have all retained in German poetry a place
which the preachers of the new Gospel themselves
never succeeded in attaining.

A similar impulse was given by the romanticists
to architecture and painting. That mediæval
tendency, which still prevailed in these
arts in the days of our youth, was their   On Art.
work. France, England, Italy themselves received
that impulse from the German romanticists,
although they were not quite conscious by what
channels it reached them. Bonald had lived in
Germany; B. Constant was as intimate with A.
W. Schlegel as Coleridge was with Tieck; and as
the whole atmosphere was pregnant with similar
tendencies, as the ground seemed only to wait for
the seed in the country of Chateaubriand and in
that of Walter Scott, it is natural enough that the
slightest germs should bear fruit. The romanticists had the merit of freeing the world from
Winckelmann's new academical theories, in which
Goethe was still entirely wrapt up, of having drawn
attention to the beauty of Gothic cathedrals, so despised in those days as barbarous *monstra*, of having

shown the value of a Giotto and a Fra Angelico, of
having made the first collections of Van Eycks and
Memlings, as they were also the first to revive the
old Catholic church music. Whatever may have
been the shortcomings of that school in Art, it
was a necessary reaction against the academical
classicism of the school of David and Canova.
However false and perilous may have been their
views about Art as an instrument for conveying
religious or other impressions, the very fact that
people began again to appreciate works of art,
which were fruits of a simple and genuine study of
nature, furthered the interests of modern Art.

　　The revival and exaggeration even of Herder's
ideas of unconscious growth in history and their
On History application to language, poetry, and law,
proper. acted most powerfully and beneficially on
the historical, if not on the natural, sciences.
The romanticists themselves self-complacently
dated a new age from their apostolic mission.
' Several of my friends and I,' said A. W. Schlegel,
candidly, ' have proclaimed in all forms, in poetry
and prose, seriously and playfully, the beginning
of a new era.' And it would be unjust not to
confess that there is some truth in this pretension.
It was only now and under their care that the

seeds sown by Herder, thirty years before, bore all their fruits. The whole history of medieval literature and language dates from them. The troubadours and the trouvères, the Minnesingers and the Meistersängers, the minstrels and jongleurs, were revived ; more than that, German philology was created by their disciples, the two Grimms. Soon neo-Latin philology was to follow; nay, even Oriental philology owes its first impulse to Fr. Schlegel's important work on the ' Wisdom of the Hindoos,' as the comparative science of languages was created by one of their generation, if not of their school, W. von Humboldt.

But we must go a step further. If their principle, applied to politics, to philosophy and natural science, has done little more than mischief; if it has led to the monstrous hypotheses of a Schelling and to his arbitrary *a priori* constructions, uncontrolled by observation of facts ; if it produced a mysticism which considered Nature as the dark mystery which the senses and understanding could never unveil, and has thus led to Oken's, Schubert's, and Steffens's scientific aberrations—it yet exercised an important influence for good in the history of philosophy, religion, legislation, the State, and even in that of science. Not only the Grimms, but

Eichhorn, Savigny, Niebuhr, Creuzer were personal friends of the romanticists, in the main adherents to their principles, and fed with their ideas. You know the revolution effected by Creuzer's 'Symbolik,' and how, in spite of all its extravagances, it created indirectly the science of comparative mythology. You also know the importance of the so-called historical school of Niebuhr and Eichhorn, Otfried Müller and Böckh, which renovated history. Even on religion their influence has been, partially at least, a salutary. If they favoured and furthered the Catholic reaction which took place after 1830 in Germany as well as in France, they have also propagated in a whole generation (from 1800 to 1830) the conviction that religion can exist without dogmas, that all inner life, all higher feeling is religion, as Schleiermacher had argued in his 'Discourses;' and in propagating this wide religion they also pleaded and furthered the cause of real, inner toleration. But their influence was most perceptible and most favourable, after all, in the awakening of national sentiment, of patriotism.

In fact, the principle according to which Art and Poetry have their roots in national life, the study of old German history, poetry, and lan-

guage at the moment when the deepest humiliation was inflicted upon the nation, the lofty
humanitarianism and idealism of a Herder, _{On National}
a Goethe, a Schiller, which seemed to have ^{Feeling.}
led to the ruin of the German State on the battle-
field of Jena, indirectly awakened the national feeling, while the persistency with which the romanticists dwelt upon the importance of nationality,
contributed not a little to the great patriotic effort
of the nation in 1813 to free itself from foreign
yoke. Nay, that peculiar national pride of a literary and scientific character, which ever since has
been proper to Germany, and which ultimately
has kindled also the national pride in things
political, can be traced to the influence of the
Romanticists. With them also began, alas, that
sort of methodical reaction in favour of feudal
and ecclesiastical institutions, which was caused
by their hatred for the radicalism and Jacobinism
of the French Revolution, its spirit of levelling
uniformity, its rationalistic spirit. It is remarkable
that the German Burke, young Gentz, made, as
early as 1796, the first German translation of
Burke's 'Reflections.' Unfortunately they did
not stop where the great interpreter of the British
Constitution stopped. They wanted to go back

not only beyond 1688, but beyond 1520; nay, further back still, to the glorious time when the holy Roman crown rested on the anointed head of the German Emperor, and his half princely, half sacerdotal sway extended over the whole of middle Europe, when the State was still entirely imbued with an ecclesiastical spirit.

The whole movement was, in fact, like that of Herder's times, a reaction against the rationalistic tendency of the eighteenth century, and

The Political Reaction.

the romanticists might be called the real executors of Herder's bequest, were it not that Herder contented himself with emancipating the mind from rationalistic conventionalism, whereas the romanticists, after having most effectually worked in the same direction, wanted to enthral it in the fetters of a worse conventionalism —that of a dead tradition, galvanised by artificial means. Herder strove to awaken the mind by appealing to all its active forces; the romanticists tried to lull it into a dreamy sleep by mesmerising as it were all those forces. Herder was of opinion that the historical principle consisted in progress; the romanticists held that it meant retrogression. Herder wished his own time to make history; the romanticists thought that they could show respect for history only by stopping its course. This they believed might be done most effectually by preaching the cause of 'throne and altar,' of authority, both secular and spiritual, in writings worthy of J. de Maistre. Almost all of them became instruments of the despotic governments of the Restoration after 1815; many of them, we have seen, were even consistent enough to throw themselves into the arms of Rome, the securest citadel, they thought, against the spirit of examination which had bred revolt and resulted in the overthrow of all the creations of history.

'The spirit of enlightenment,' said A. W. Schlegel, 'which has no respect whatever for darkness, is the most decided and most dangerous adversary of poetry.' Now, as poetry was supposed to penetrate the whole life, public and private, the consequence was that enlightenment in the eyes of the romanticists was an enemy to be combated also in the domains of Religion and the State. Hence their strong antipathy for the French Revolution, which Klopstock, Kant, Schiller, and even Herder had saluted as the beginning of a new era. They saw in it nothing but Voltaireanism and the worship of the goddess Reason; the presumptuous attempt to create mechanically a

s

social order according to rationalistic principles;
the negation, in a word, of History. Unfortunately their medieval tastes were not so inno-
cent as the children's play with the bells spoken
of by Goethe. The literary and philosophical tendencies of earlier times soon developed into political and ecclesiastical tendencies. Alexander of
Russia was deeply imbued with their ideas when
he formed the ' Holy Alliance,' more even against
the spirit of the past century than against revolutionary France. In Austria and in Italy the
governments made themselves the champions of
the Roman Church ; in France ' throne and altar '
formed an alliance against scepticism and liberalism; the petty nobility of Germany already dreamed
of a restoration of its feudal rights; Prussian
professors and statesmen began to vie with each
other in theorising on the ' Christo-Teutonic '
State. It was reserved for the most exalted disciple
of the romanticists to realise their ideal—so far as
the good old Protestant State of Prussia allowed
him to realise it—when he at last ascended the
throne in 1840 : for Germany's favourable star had
granted a long life to his wise and good father.
Romanticism, indeed, was long dead, when Frederick William IV., the ' Romanticist on the

throne,' as Strauss called him by *innuendo* in a celebrated pamphlet, delivered up to the Catholic Church the rights of the State, so strenuously defended by his father, catholicised Protestantism as much as it lay in his power, and tried to create artificially a medieval constitution. He did not succeed; but Germany still pays the penalty of these dangerous poetical experiments.

We have arrived at the end of our task. Germany has not since been idle. She has produced one poet of genius and many of talent since 1825. She has given to the world some great scientific and historical works, Conclusion. which are unequalled even in the period we have been studying together. Some great discoveries have been made in natural science; but no new and fruitful ideas, such as had come forth from Germany during the sixty or seventy years we have been contemplating, have been produced. No new science has been created. The German intellect has been busy, ever since Goethe's death, in developing or contradicting, in modifying or applying the ideas propounded and insisted on by the three generations to which Germany owes her intellectual Renaissance, the generation of 1760, that of 1780, and that of 1800. We have

s 2

examined together these ideas, and I need not
dwell upon them longer—or if I were to do so, I
should be obliged to ask you for fifty meetings
more—but I must beg you to bear in mind (what
is indeed the purport of all these lectures), that
the point of view, which was the general one in
Europe during the last fifty years, was really
opened by Germany.

Let us not be misled by the universality of
certain currents of thought as to their origin.
When all Europe seemed bent on the mechanical
explanation of nature, when Galileo, Kepler, Descartes, devoted their lives to this task, it was
England which, through Harvey, Gilbert, Bacon,
gave the impulse, which, through Hobbes, Newton,
Locke, kept the lead in the movement which had
sprung up in this island.

It was the same with the French thought of
the past century. No sooner had the Montes-
quieus and Voltaires, the Rousseaus and Diderots,
expressed their ideas, than these ideas passed
into European currency and were changed into
foreign coin. The same phenomenon may be
seen in the successive phases of the period during which Germany was acquiring the intellectual
hegemony, *i.e.* from about 1763 to about 1830.

Scarcely had Winckelmann declared war against the reigning *rococo*, than all over Europe sculpture, painting, and architecture took the new classical turn. When, fifty years later, a reaction set in against the *style empire*, which had but been an exaggeration of Winckelmann's theories, when Chateaubriand in France, and Walter Scott in England, brought the Middle Ages into fashion, they only followed—unconsciously of course—the impulse given by the German romanticists. It was the same with the more important movement which took place all over Europe in historical and natural science.

Not only would Augustin Thierry and Thomas Carlyle have been impossible without the German revolution of thought; but the way in which our century looks upon antiquity, so widely different from that in which Pope or Voltaire looked upon it, was opened by Winckelmann and Lessing. The point of view, if not the method, which is generally accepted now in natural science, was first held by Goethe. The historical sciences—under which name we comprise not only political and literary history, but also theology, philology, archæology, and jurisprudence—have been, during the whole century, and have scarcely even now ceased to be,

under the empire of Herder's ideas of evolution.
Comparative philology, whether we consider it
a branch of natural or of historical science, has
not yet abandoned the roads opened by W. von
Humboldt and Bopp, nor have the neo-Latin
studies repudiated the paternity of Diez, or the Ger-
manistic that of Grimm.   A new basis for philosophy has been laid by Kant.   Schiller's conception of art has been more and more generally
adopted.   The science of religion, and the independent spirit in which our time treats the history
of Christianity, so different from the aggressive
tone of the last century, are mainly due to
Herder's German disciples.   Above all, the consciousness with which individualism—a conservative principle, when understood in the German
sense—still resists here and there the overwhelm-
ing tide of the levelling tendencies of our days,
is of German origin.   So also is the consciousness with which the right of intuitive genius—
an aristocratic principle—is as yet maintained
against the all-invading method of analysis and
rationalism, a method which, in its ultimate results, must always further the democratic interest,
as it applies to the most general of human faculties.
The fact of this struggle would suffice to prove

that the main principles of German thought have
not triumphed without contest in Europe. They
can hardly be said to have triumphed even in
Germany, where they have been deeply modified
and corrected by new currents, just as they had
themselves deeply modified and corrected the
English French currents of the past.

EPILOGUE.

THE romanticists were men 'who, with the weapons forged by the age of enlightenment, combated enlightenment itself, in the domains of science, art, morality, and politics.' With these words one of the most gifted Young Hegelians, who rose against romanticism towards 1830, Arnold Ruge, characterised his opponents. The exaggeration, in fact, of the romantic movement produced, as will always be the case, a strong reaction. This reaction took place in every department of intellectual life, just as the romantic movement had pervaded every branch of activity. The historical idea had been carried so far that it had led to the justification of every abuse and of every crime of the good old time, nay, to plans and efforts for bringing the world back to that good old time.

Hegel himself did not go to such lengths. He remained throughout faithful to the ideal of the modern State and the Protestant religion. Feudality and Catholicism re- Hegel, 1770-1831. mained always for him things of the past, which no effort could recall to life; but he saw in the bureaucratical State of Frederick William III. the crowning result of all the historical evolutions, the end to which all the political history of Germany had tended. He regarded the 'Evangelical Alliance' of Frederick William III. as destined to bring together Calvinists and Lutherans, as the ultimate expression of the religious development of his country. Now this evolution was, according to the philosophy of identity, which he had modified, but not abandoned, nothing but the evolution of universal reason itself, as developed in time and space; and he gave to this view its philosophical formula, when he declared that 'whatever is, is reasonable, and whatever is reasonable, is '—a proposition quite defensible if only Hegel's premiss were accepted, that *his* dialectic method was a thinking process identical with the process of things which in its turn was but the process of eternal thought thinking itself. For Hegel had given to the *fieri* idea of Herder dialectic and metaphysical form: the 'immanent negativity' of things—everything is always changing, consequently denies itself unceasingly—is the form of a thought, which is identical with the process of *fieri* in the world of phenomena. In the same way he had undertaken to prove that Christianity had given expression to the consciousness of the absolute in its purest form—as far as imagination and feeling were concerned—that it was consequently *the* absolute religion, as his philosophy was of course *the* absolute philosophy. At last he had gone so far as to interpret all the different dogmas of Christianity so as to make of them symbols of his own philosophy.

This provoked the rebellion of his most eminent disciples. Strauss and Feuerbach, B. Bauer and Ruge, separated from him, and formed the left wing of Hegelianism, or, as they called themselves, the Young-Hegelians. Strauss attacked supernaturalism as well as theological rationalism with the weapons of historical investigation in his 'Life of Jesus,' which appeared in 1835. Faithful to Hegel's earlier ideas he presented in this memorable book the origin of Christianity as growing naturally out of the thoughts, feelings, and circumstances of the time, not as created by

one stroke of a magic wand. He showed how far
legend, myth, and the popular imagination had
aided in the birth of Christianity, combating
the supernatural as well as the rationalistic explanation of the miracles ; but combating quite as
warmly the irreverent theories of the eighteenth
century, which saw only wonder-workers and impostors in all founders of religions. He thus became, together with F. C. Baur, who had begun
before him and who continued his work, the father
of the new theological school, known as the Tübingen school, whilst Feuerbach subjected more fully
the theoretical side of Hegel's doctrine to the
dialectical process which he had learned from his
master, investigating the essence of religion in
general ; and soon a numerous school of young
thinkers followed in his steps. A return to common-
sense in philosophy, to criticism in theology, was
the consequence of these attacks against the high-
priest of ' official ' philosophy. Even in the field of
pagan mythology the spirit of enlightenment rose
once more against the spirit of dusky divination ;
and Voss and Lobeck threw down the gauntlet to
Creuzer in the name of common-sense and reason.

Something similar took place in jurisprudence
and history proper. Savigny as well as Eichhorn

had taught that our time had neither vocation nor aptitude for law-giving; that all fertile legislation The re-awakening of rational-ism. was the work of generations; that the Roman law, which still lived in all the countries of the Continent, the German law, which still prevailed in England, were only the expression of national spirit, custom, tradition, and local necessities. Already in Hegel's lifetime his most eloquent disciple, Gans, had defended against the historical school the rights of the living, and with these the rights also of reason. At the same time the wonderful development of the Frederician and Napoleonic legislation seemed the living refutation of the historic theory, pushed as far as it was pushed by the romanticists. Not a generation had passed away since the great work of Bonaparte; and the *Code Napoléon* seemed already ineradicably rooted in France. Nay, with an eye of envy non-Prussian Germany regarded this simple rational legislation as contrasted with her own various complicated and antiquated laws. Napoleon, after all, had made his *Code civil* as well as his *Code pénal* and his *Code de procédure*—as Frederick II. had, thirty years before, constructed his less comprehensive *Landrecht*—out of the fragments of former historical legislation, just as his new administration was only that of the old monarchy in disguise. This, however, was not yet well recognised by the generation of 1830, which was still persuaded that all this new organisation had sprung out of the Emperor's head, like Minerva from that of Jupiter, and that he had shaped it exclusively according to abstract principles of justice and utility. In all German universities 'natural law,' *i.e.* the rationalistic theory of law, as the eighteenth century had preached it ever since Thomasius, again mounted the professors' chairs and revindicated the rights of reason against the absolutism of the historic school, which Goethe had so wittily parodied by anticipation.

Like an inveterate disease, law and rights descend trailing from generation to generation, and gently move from place to place. Reason becomes non-sense ; what was a blessing is a curse. Woe to thee that thou art a grandson ! Of those rights, alas ! with which we are born, there is ne'er a question.

A large body of historians followed the road of the new rationalistic school of jurisprudence. Germany was inundated with histories which treated all the past with reference to the present, which were not content to tell the facts, but commented upon them from the point

History.

of view of the French liberals or the French re-
publicans of the day. Rotteck's and Welcker's
great 'Dictionary of Political Science,' entirely
written under the influence of formal French
constitutionalism, was the Bible of the new
liberal doctrinaires, who sprang up everywhere in
Germany and repeated in the small Chambers of
Carlsruhe and Darmstadt the great oratorical
tournaments of Paris under the Restoration and
Louis Philippe. If the most practical of English
statesmen, Lord Palmerston, naïvely believed
that the recipe of a parliamentary constitution,
neatly written on white paper, would work in
Spain and Greece, as that growth of centuries,
the British constitution, worked in England, the
German professors of 1830 were certainly excus-
able in thinking that they might introduce that
most delicate and most abnormal form of government into their tiny bureaucratical States. Had
not the French constitution-mongers, with Ben-
jamin Constant at their head, adapted it to Continental use?

There was, however, a party which went
further than the constitutionalists. 'Young
Germany'—so we call the group of youthful
writers, born about 1810, who, towards 1830, trod

in the footsteps of Börne and Heine—Young Germany did not stop at representative monarchy, as
it did not stop at Deism in philosophy, Young
although Heine himself remained ever Germany.
faithful to the theory of a limited monarchy, and
came back at the end of his life to 'the simple
belief in the personal God of the common man,' as
he used to say. Laube and Gutzkow, Wienbarg
and Ruge attacked Christianity and even Hegelianism, in which they had been bred, with the violence
of the French revolutionists of 1792. They showed
a determined predilection for atheism and materialism in philosophy, for Jacobinism in politics;
they even preached, with the Saint-Simonians, the
emancipation of woman and the abolition of individual property. They called themselves proudly
'modern' minds. They protested against all
forms of aristocracy, social as well as intellectual.
The State was to become the one all-regulating
power; not the historical State, as it had grown
up in the course of centuries—but the modern
State built up according to the dictates of Reason
—or of Jean-Jacques; not even the State of 1790,
but the democratical State of 1793. The place
held till now by the great—kings, aristocrats, geniuses—was to be held henceforward by the people,

which was to become the hero of history and public
life. At the same time they claimed, not only for
the people, but for themselves, the right to material
enjoyment, even to luxury; not an equality in
misery, but an equality in wealth was their unattainable ideal. Their religion was the rehabilitation of the flesh; science and poetry were means
for preaching and propagating their new gospel.
Their last and most dangerous disciple, Ferdinand
Lassalle, died only fifteen years ago, not without
having left his fatal legacy to Germany.

Börne and Heine, who had given the first
signal for this reaction in favour of rationalism
against history, and of French ideas
against German, did not, as I said, go so
far. Heine was too much of an artist not to be
shocked by such excesses; Börne too much of a
Stoic to go such lengths—his ideal was the in-
corruptible Robespierre, not the epicurean Danton.
For Heine, politics, as well as religion, history,
philosophy, never ceased to be themes for poetical
variations. In reality they were as indifferent to
him as the religious subjects of the great works of
the Italian Renaissance were indifferent to the
artists who produced them. It was Börne and
Heine, nevertheless, who set the example. Heine

himself had belonged, as I have said, to the
romantic school, and was the personal pupil of A.
W. Schlegel. He had begun with two romantic tra-
gedies which exhibit only too visibly the traces of
the master's influence; and he was destined to give
in 'Atta Troll' and the 'Romanzero' what the
romanticists themselves had never been able to
give, the ideal romantic poem. There was not
even wanting in them the much recommended
irony of Fred. Schlegel. But Heine had always
been a somewhat unruly disciple. As early as at
the age of sixteen he had sung his song of the
Napoleonic grenadiers, which was in opposition to
the whole tendency of his masters; and you know
how he developed the theme of the Napoleon-
worship in the incomparable prose-poem of
'Tambour Legrand.' Now, for a while Germany
neglected Heine the immortal poet for Heine
the ephemeral politician and philosopher—there
are many foreigners who do so still—and was led
to accept the most meagre of doctrines by the
irresistible fascination of a prose and a verse which
she had not heard since the great days of Goethe
and Schiller; whilst Börne's incomparable wit
made her forget for a time that his political ideal
was still more shallow than that of Heine.

T

We have seen that the liberating movement of
1813, the rising of the whole nation against the
foreign yoke, had taken place under the inspiration of romanticism. It had taken the form of
a crusade, not only against Napoleon and the
French, but against the rationalism, the democracy, and the cosmopolitan pretences of the eighteenth century and the great Revolution. It had
invoked the Christian and religious spirit, Teutonic
patriotism, feudal loyalty towards the hereditary
princes ; and these feelings were still very strong
when Heine and Börne, towards 1825, gave expression to the aspirations of the rising generation which had not felt the hardship of foreign
oppression and to which the political reality
which had followed the enthusiastic rise of 1813,
had proved a source of the bitterest disappoint-
ment. The shameless despotism of the fathers of
the fatherland, most of them of Napoleon's own
creation, or at least promotion, the petty tyranny
of their instruments, and the religious fanaticism
or hypocrisy which already began to spring up in
the official spheres of South Germany, were quite
sufficient to alienate the young from the romantic
cause. It was the time when Grabbe wrote his
tragedy of 'The Hundred Days,' when Zedlitz

composed his poem of the dead Cæsar's ' Midnight
Review,' when W. Müller's ' Griechenlieder,' and
Mosen's Polish songs resounded in the streets of
every German town. The reaction in favour of
cosmopolitism and humanitarianism against patriotic one-sidedness, and of French sympathies
against German national prejudices, was at the
same time a partial return to the ideas which had
predominated in Germany in the times of Schiller
and Goethe, and the exposition of which has been
the main object of these lectures. A partial
return, I say ; for in opposing democracy to aristocracy, the masses to individualism, the mechanical making of states and laws to the ideas of
growth and evolution, it was in contradiction
with the creed of Herder and of Goethe. In its
cosmopolitism and in its paganism it was quite
under the sway of the great Humanitarian and the
great Heathen.

The Francophil, democratical, and rationalistic
current, initiated by Börne, Heine, and Young
Germany, prevailed for nearly a quarter Little
of a century, from 1825 to 1850. Then Germany.
again under the influence of the disenchantment
which the failures of 1848 had caused, and still
more. under the impressions produced by the

T 2

bankruptcy of the French democracy in 1849, a contrary current arose in Germany.

Already towards 1840 this new current had set in: the current of German national spirit Its national against foreign influence, and above character. all against France. From 1840 to 1848 the 'Germanistenversammlungen' or meetings of Teutonic philologists, jurisconsults and historians, were for Germany what the scientific congresses were for Italy, the pretext and opportunity for asserting and preparing the unity of Germany. For it was written that our political ideas should be framed by professors, as professors had framed our literary and artistic, our religious and philosophical ideas. The two men, however, who gave us, the one a national poetry, the other a national state, were not professors: but could they have done their work if the professors had not prepared the ground for them? Would they not have done it in a still more satisfactory way if the professors had not continued to interfere in it?

The outbreak of French *Chauvinism*—the ugly word seems to have established itself in all our languages—and the thirst for conquest betrayed in 1840, the cries for the Rhine which resounded in Paris, as soon as Europe was threatened with a general war through the complication in the East, contributed not a little to strengthen this current, particularly in the menaced provinces of the left bank, which had been the special centre of the romantic movement. This current is, nevertheless, very distinct from that of 1813, and it became still more so after 1848, when the romantic dreams of a resurrection of Frederick Barbarossa's Empire, under the form of a Seventy-Millions Germany, prevented the foundation of the national State. It was, in the main, undoubtedly directed against what was un-German in the political rationalism of ' Young Germany '—whose best men, from Börne, Gans, and Heine, down to F. Lassalle, were, curious to say, really not of German blood, being Israelites by birth, if not by creed. The declaration of war itself was a violent pamphlet against Börne from the pen of Gervinus.

Nevertheless, the reaction of 1850 did not affect a picturesque and poetical costume like that of 1813. The new patriots deemed it unnecessary and childish to show the love of their country by their white collars, bare necks, and long hair. On the contrary, they affected rather a sort of bourgeois common-place exterior. They dreaded to be considered as unpractical dreamers; their highest ambition was to be taken for 'positive' people. Their ideal in history was the honest, stedfast, prosy *Bürger* of the sixteenth century, not the romantic knight of the Middle Ages, or the Germanic chieftain of barbarous times. They saw the strength of the nation in the middle-class, and turned against the *Junker* nobility, as well as against the democratic masses. They did not dream of a traditional royalty, but of a monarchy resting on contract like that of England since 1688. They showed no sympathy for the Church or for any religious mysticism, such as had inspired the poets of 1813; on the contrary, they wished to impress upon men's minds that they were Protestants—sober, unpoetical Protestants— and at the same time the heirs of Kant, whose purely moral religion, without dogmas and forms of worship, was to be the German religion *par excellence*, *i.e.* the final form of Protestantism, as for the English Deists of the past century Uni-tarianism was the final form of English Pro-testantism.

But if they were disciples of Kant the moralist, they pointedly ignored Kant the metaphysician. 'Young Germany' had still been strongly imbued with the speculative spirit; it had grown up under

Hegel's, as yet, uncontested rule. The new school deliberately turned their backs on all metaphysics : during their reign over public opinion, if not over State and Church—*i.e.* from 1850 to about 1866—a sort of indiffer- Its Positive Character in Science. entism, nay, of aversion, for philosophical specula- tion seemed to have taken hold of the nation, awakened, as she was, and sobered down from her metaphysical excesses. Even in their way of treat- ing science they went to the opposite extreme. The great advantage of Kant's influence was, that science during the first half of this century was always handled in a philosophical spirit. There was certainly an excess both in the so-called 'philo- sophy of nature' and in the 'philosophy of history,' which interfered too often with the sober and exact observation and verification of facts. The new school assumed to be more positive. General ideas had nothing to do with science ; and they even went so far as to treat history as a sort of exact science. The famous 'German method' dates from this time. Imagination, and even intuition, were banished from historical studies, as well as from natural science. Facts alone were to be sought for, sifted, and assembled ; the only combination of the facts which was allowed was connexion

through cause and effect; and the disciples were
so well drilled that they succeeded at last not
only in finding the facts they wanted, and in making them take the appearance which they desired,
but in driving life itself out of history, which is
but the evolution of life. Even the present generation, which has come back to long neglected philosophy, is animated in its researches by a spirit
entirely different from that which predominated in
the times of Hegel. It is, indeed, Kant's criticism
of reason with its strictly experimental character
and its opposition to all *a priori* speculation, which
our matter-of-fact juniors have taken up again.
In other words they have returned to the point
whence their fathers started on their strange
Odyssey, and they are favoured in their new
voyage by all the light which the progress of
natural science, accomplished in the interval,
throws on their road. And not the professional
philosophers alone, but the men of science themselves, the physiologists especially, tread now with
a surer foot in the steps of the great renovator of
modern thought.

If, however, the men of 1850 repudiated all
philosophical ideas, they did not reject political
ideas; nay, history soon became in their hands a

storehouse of arguments for political views. The
' men of Gotha'—so they were called in consequence
of the Gotha Parliament of 1849, in which they
formed the majority—thought, if they did not
say, that politics alone really deserved to
occupy a nation which had come of age.
In Politics.
They were staunch Liberals of the constitutional
school; but their ideal was the old English Constitution, not the French one of 1830.   In general
their leaders, from Dahlmann and Gervinus, down
to Gneist and Waitz, Sybel and Häusser, were
decidedly English in their sympathies, until—
well, until a period which lies beyond the limits
of the subject which I have to treat here.

Like the English Liberals of the old school they
had arrived at a species of compromise between
political rationalism and ' historicism.' They still
adhered to the German idea of evolution—the
only great German idea to which they remained
faithful—but they corrected it consciously, as the
English had done and do almost unconsciously, by
adaptation of the past to the exigencies of the
present.   They saw the historical spirit, not in a
return to the past, or in a stopping of history at
a given moment, but in continuous progress.
Moreover, as, although mostly professors, they

claimed to be practical politicians, not dreamers
and theorists, they did not want to awaken Frederick Barbarossa in his Kyffhäuser, and call to life
the 'Holy Roman Empire of the German Nation,'
with its seventy millions of souls and its sway over
Hungary and Italy, Poland and Burgundy. They
wanted to have a national State strong enough to
defend itself against foreign aggression, not so
mighty as to arouse the fears or suspicion of the
neighbouring nations; a State similar to those
founded, or at least perfected, by Louis XI. of
France, Henry VII. of England, Ferdinand the
Catholic of Spain. In consequence they raised
a characteristic protest against the Othos and
Fredericks of the Middle Ages, who, instead of
following the sensible and moderate national policy
of Henry I., went to assume in Rome the crown
of the Cæsars. And as Austria was still considered, and considered herself as the natural
heir of the Holy Empire, as her possessions lay to
a great extent outside the frontiers of the German
language and German interests; as she was Catholic throughout, the exclusion of Austria became
an article, and indeed the chief article of the new
political faith. Thence the name of the party,
'Little Germany,' as opposed to these successors

of the romantic school still numerous in 1848, who
wanted to defend the German interests 'on the
Mincio,' and saw in Austria the champion of
German grandeur, and were usually called the
party of 'Great Germany.'

The 'Little Germans,' indeed, saw clearly from
the beginning, in Protestant Prussia, the power
which was to realise the longed-for national State,
powerful enough to defend its integrity, but without any hankering after political hegemony in
Europe such as Charles V. and Louis XIV. had
aspired to, and such as had always haunted the
patriots of 1813, when they dreamed of avenging
the death of young Conradin and restoring the
Empire of his grandfather. Their aim, I said,
was to be eminently matter-of-fact, and they
affected a contempt for high-flown or sentimental
ideas, which was often taken abroad for less of a
fanfaronnade de vice than it really was. They were
so anxious to show that they were no longer
modest, shy, dreamy sentimentalists that they
sometimes overdid it; for they strove not only
against the looseness of moral principles, the
Bohemian life, the Jacobinism and the Frenchified
ways of 'Young Germany,' to whose Gallic
frivolity they opposed their Teutonic earnestness;

not only against the mania for poetical fancy-costumes, and the unpractical enthusiasm of the patriots of 1813. They strove also against the idealism of Goethe's and Schiller's time, against its exaggerated individualism, against the eternal self-education, against the whole worship of beautiful souls, against its humanitarian cosmopolitism, and absence of prejudice ; but above all against its alienation from public life, and its exclusive admiration of art and thought as the highest activity of man.

Gervinus, at the end of his history of German poetry, which appeared from 1835 to 1842, and was a species of patriotic pamphlet in five huge volumes, breaks out into these words, which give vent to the suppressed idea, that pervades his whole book, as it was the undercurrent of the feelings of his whole generation :

Is it not time to use the forces hidden in the nation ? to ask the governments to appreciate those forces, and give them free course ? to wish that the nation, which forms the centre and nucleus of Europe, should come out of the despised position which it occupies ? that it should enter at last on its majority ? . . . But, by whatever means that aim is to be attained, it is not by the ways which our poetry has taken. . . . We want a man of Luther's stamp. He himself was tempted to undertake the task ; but he despaired for the ever alleged reason that he did not believe in the political intelligence and capacity of his nation. If it were in the nature of the people, he was of opinion, it would show itself without laws. . . . But we will not despair of this people. . . . We cannot believe that a nation can have achieved so great results in poetry, religion, art, and science, and yet should be absolutely incapable of any political achievement. . . . Our duty is to understand the signs of the times, to give up scattering our strength as we do, to direct our activity towards the point which is the object of the most ardent desires of all. The fight on the field of art is over; now we ought to aim steadily at the other object, which nobody as yet amongst us has attained. Perhaps Apollo will there also grant us the prize, which he has not refused us elsewhere!

The 'man of Luther's stamp' came, and the first to turn his back upon him was the man who had yearned for him; and the man of Luther's stamp saw what Luther had seen, that political capacity was not in the nature of the nation, and so, having vainly tried to build the national State with the help of the nation, he. at last did it without the nation. As soon as he had done his work, the 'Little Germans,' who had not understood him, and had opposed him, loaded him with praise, for they saw that it was *their* dream which he had realised. So he called them again to work with him to fit up the new building, and they put their hand to the work, and again proved that political capacity was not in their nature, and thus they separated again, perhaps for ever.

Nevertheless, they have been, and are, trying hard to become a political nation. To arrive at this result, Germany, freed for the last fifty years from all social, religious, and national prejudices, had to acquire them again artificially, or at least to form a new 'cake of custom,' or *ensemble* of such prejudices as were necessary for the practical purposes of a national and political life. A man who sees all sides of a question, whom the passions of the patriot and the party-man do not move, who thinks more of being let alone than of acting upon others, a man without prejudices—in a word, the ideal man of Goethe's time—was scarcely fit for the new task. For this work, good, solid, narrow, social and other prejudices were a necessity. The consolidation then of prejudices, above all, of the national prejudice, was the chief, though unconscious aim of the German intellectual movement since 1850; and as regards national prejudice, they certainly succeeded. Whenever national interests

Its influence on German thought.

are at stake, we all hold together, as our fathers
never did, and show a public spirit utterly unknown to them. I cannot say the same as yet in
cases where the interests of liberty, of good administration, of free trade, and so forth, are concerned.
It is a great thing that at least in national questions, we should be united and unanimous even
to excess. As I said in my last lecture, the death
of individualism, which we have witnessed since
1850, seems a contradiction of *the* German idea.
Still, it was necessary to a certain degree, because
excessive individualism unfits man for public life.

One of the first means of creating those prejudices, and one of its last consequences, was the
creation of national pride, a virtue or a vice,
utterly unknown to the great period of 1790.
This new patriotism had not the simplicity of
the French or Greek patriotism, which regards
all other nations as barbarians ; nor the humble
and sentimental tenderness of Italian patriotism,
which clings to the redeemed country as a mother
does to a child saved from death but still delicate
and ailing, and scarcely able to face the hard-
ships of life in a public school with hardy com-
rades. It had not the robust vigour of the Roman
and old-English patriotism, which simply ignored

the legal existence of all who were not Roman citizens or British subjects. The new German patriotism, which is not to be confounded with the old Prussian, was not, and is not *naïf*. It is conscious; it is intentional; it has a tincture of pedantry because it has been made by scholars and literary men. It has sprung up from a feeling of *want* of patriotism, such as had reigned before, and against which reaction was necessary. It resembles in that respect the religion of the German romanticists, who had all been free-thinkers, and resolved one fine day to become believers because belief was a necessary basis of all poëtical excellence. Hence the exaggerations of German patriotism. It was not born naturally, or spontaneously,'it was the fruit of reflection.

It was not the less justified for all that; for it was really necessary for the creation of a national State. Now, next to a just and righteous order, which is the very *raison d'être* of the State, national independence and national strength, which guarantees this independence, are the most indispensable conditions for the welfare of a nation. When a nation does not possess these, it must sacrifice everything to attain them, even liberty. The Spaniards gave the example of it in the

beginning of this century, because they had at
least this superiority over Germany, that they
possessed a national State—worse, certainly, than
the one which the French wanted to force upon
them—but still a national State. This goal once
attained, the struggle for internal liberty ought
to begin, with its various vicissitudes of victory
and defeat, as England carried it on from the
destruction of the Armada to the reign of
George IV. ; and it is only when this conquest
has been achieved, that the nation can allow
herself again the luxury of such liberal ideas
and feelings as those which animated the great
founders of German culture.

Meanwhile those ideas bear fruit a thousand-
fold throughout the world, and spring up even in
distant fields, whither the seed has been
carried by the winds of history. But at $\qquad$ Conclusion.
home there still remains, and will ever remain a
quiet, unobserved community of the faithful, who
guard devotedly the treasure bequeathed to their
country by the great heroes of thought and art.
They live outside the strife of public life, looking
on it sometimes with regret, sometimes with
anger—but always with hope. They will not allow
that Germany, which has given to the world the

ideas of Lessing and Herder, of Goethe and Schiller, should for ever exclude them from their national creed. They will take care that, when the day is come, Germany shall restore those wide ideas to their place of honour at the hearth from which they went forth over the world. When that moment is come, Germany, which now seems chiefly occupied with the selfish, though necessary, task of strengthening her house against the storms which might threaten it, and of rendering it more habitable than it has been before, will, I for one am confident, resume with undivided heart her share in that common work of Europe which, under whatever national form it may be produced, is the civilisation of mankind.

INDEX.

www.ingramcontent.com/pod-product-compliance
Lightning Source LLC
Chambersburg PA
CBHW020931120726
47905CB00008B/2473